RUN Baby Jake

Printed in the United States of America
First printing: July, 2005
Most recent printing indicated by the last digit below:
7   6   5   4   3   2   1

Published by
MERTON GLENN PUBLISHING HOUSE
1527 South Union Road
Cedar Falls, Iowa 50613
Phone: 319-277-1904
orders@runbabyjake.com

www.runbabyjake.com

RUN Baby Jake

By Jill Carlson

Merton Glenn
Publishing House

Jake lay dozing: knees drawn up — hands beneath his chin. The warmth of his water bed surrounded him. Little gurgling sounds lapped around him like a blanket.

Deep inside his slumber, little voices played. His mother's: silky soft — singing absently; the radio's low monotone; twilight birds in endless primal calls.

Into the soothing sleep sounds . . . the creak of a door . . . the soft wheedling voice of his grandmother. Jake turned fitfully. His stomach tightened. His legs curled up in fear.

Then, his mama's voice: "What are you saying? No! I won't listen to this! It can't be. When did Doctor Quaid say that? No. *No!*" Jake felt his bed shaking. "Why didn't he tell *me* instead of *you!?*"

In Jake's half-sleep, voices floated. Slow whines rose up to meet crescendo shrieks.

"I don't want him to die! He CAN'T!"

A door slammed. Shock waves ripped through his body. His mama's soft sobbing pierced his soul. Half-dreaming, half-waking, Jake cried out.

———————

The sun was settling low into the sky when the phone rang. Dr. Benjamin Quaid groaned against his pillow. He let it ring five times, then wrestled it from its cradle.

"Quaid."

"*Doctor* Quaid?" A slow, soft drawl.

"Who . . . is this?" But he knew.

"Well, Benjamin." The voice was throaty, lazy. "I can call back."

But Quaid was fully awake, tiny bumps prickling his arms.

"S'okay."

What does she want?

"I need . . . some advice about a medical matter."

Silence.

"You owe me, Benjamin."

Quaid sank down in the bed, squeezing the receiver until his whole body shook.

"You know, Benjamin, a friendly chat in your office would be good right now . . . don't you think?"

I don't think. I can't think. No, please no. Not again. God, not again. Quaid cleared his throat. "Okay . . . okay. . . . Forty minutes. I'll be there." He clicked the phone onto its cradle and leaned against the pillow like a dead man.

Quiet. The room had emptied itself of sound. So quiet that Doctor Benjamin Quaid heard the muffled footsteps of his wife as she turned away from the door and padded down the carpeted hallway.

———————

Helene Morrow rested her hand on the phone and smiled. She looked with pleasure at her teakwood paneled walls, the rich Moroccan tapestries. Absently she studied an oxen figurine on her desk. She reached out one tapered finger and touched its horns.

I have waited long for this. . . . It will be so very sweet.

All in one package. So . . . poetic.

The silver phone warbled softly. Still smiling, Helene tucked her hair behind one ear and picked up the receiver.

Slowly she drawled her famous greeting: "Morrow Imports. It's never too late for treasure."

The phone erupted in violent obscenities, then simmered to a stiletto tirade: "Helene! My little package from Turkey is still hung up in New York. Knock some sense into your guy at Customs and earn your commission!"

Helene's jaw clenched, then relaxed. Her eyes glinted green fire while she breathed deeply and quietly. Then she poured on the sugar. "Furman, honey. Don't upset yourself. You'll get your little Turkish delights."

"Just do it!" Furman Adams breathed steadily into his phone. Helene waited, tensing. She knew what was coming.

"What are we going to do about that other thing?"

Helene steadied her voice. "It's . . . taken care of."

Silence. Then a click.

Helene gentled the phone onto the cradle, her breath coming in short, uneven gasps.

"Your Honor Mister Furman Adams," she muttered. "Big man. *Big* man. You may be the mayor of Cedar Bend, but you will *not* share a grandchild with me."

She patted her hair back into place and glided across the dense, creamy carpet.

Opening the teakwood door, she walked into the anteroom and pulled it quietly behind her. Time to keep the appointment.

Late. Tony was late. Again. He cranked the stereo and jammed his foot on the accelerator. Thirty-two — thirty-three. Maybe thirty-four and slide through that yellow light. Can't get nailed again. Just stay under thirty-five.

Ease behind the rusted Chevy — burst of speed in front of the Escort. Slide easy now. No squeals, no attention. Tony raked his hands through curly black hair and tapped one foot to the stereo. *Love ya, Baby, all the ti-ime.*

He lurched into the hospital driveway and scanned frantically for a sliver of space. Parking spot. Grab it. Squeeze ahead of that powder-blue Porsche. It's yours. Jam the pedal, kid. Three minutes late. They'll let it go one more time.

Tony's Jeep oiled into the tiny parking space and got an angry blast from the Porsche. He turned off the key and vaulted out the door in one fluid motion, threading himself through parked cars and into the main door of Shannon Memorial, jean jacket flapping, Reeboks squeaking. Grab that time clock before it shows five after eight. Tony squirmed through the revolving door and shot for the elevator.

"Whoa!" He rammed the tweed-coated Benjamin Quaid and spun him around. "Hey man, Sorry! You okay?" He steadied the doctor's huge frame, then shot into the elevator just ahead of the closing doors.

He breathed deeply and punched the button. It was always the same: The rush to the hospital every evening, the silent elevator ride to his maintenance cubicle — the long night patching together the mechanical bowels of Shannon Memorial.

One long groan from the elevator as the doors opened. Tony sighed and got out at the basement.

Helene Morrow crossed her trim ankles and sat stiffly in the corner armchair. Her pale skin caught the fading light from the window, and her smooth hair framed a stoic face. Black linen followed the contours of her body, a stark contrast to the white arms. The only movement was in her half-lidded eyes which followed Dr. Benjamin Quaid's weary entrance through the office door.

Ben paused in the doorway and glanced sharply at the woman in the corner. Once he had loved that austere face and body — adored every movement of those cat-green eyes. Now he choked with fear at the sight of her. He felt clumsy near her cool serenity, never in control of his arms and legs. He caught his shoe on the carpet, then quickly straightened and cleared his throat.

He muttered a greeting. "Good to see you, Helene."

"No it's not."

Ben's shoulder twitched. "Well. . . ." He eased himself into the leather sofa, his giant frame folding into supple cushions. There was a pause while he sized her up, then a heavy sigh of resignation. "Go ahead, Helene. Get it over with."

Helene's lips parted and she drew a quick deep breath.

"It's payback time."

One finger on her left hand raised slightly on the chair arm, then settled.

Ben shifted uneasily, wrenching his focus from the cat eyes. He studied the miniature gilded clock on his desk in morbid fascination. Marta had given it to him on their anniversary, and it had kept perfect time for ten long years. The little gold-etched roman numerals caught the late evening sun from the bay window, and he stared at it for a few moments, hoping for inspiration.

There was no sound at all except the ticking of the tiny pendulum, which filled the room like a beating heart.

"Be glad I'm alive, Ben." The soft accusation cracked through the silence like a rifle shot. Helene smiled coldly, showing even white teeth and a flash of pink tongue.

Her eyes focused unblinking on Ben's face. He wiped damp hands roughly on his tweed coat.

Helene twitched her nose a bit and sat back in triumph, waiting. The clock ticked its relentless, regular beats. Somewhere Ben heard an elevator door open.

"Marianna is in need of your skill, Ben." Her look was viperous, exultant.

"Marianna? I know. She's been . . . in to see me . . . she. . . ." He paused, alarmed at the glint in Helene's eyes.

"Do a little math, Ben. One plus one makes two." She waited, motionless. "And we don't want two. Do we."

Ben blanched, feeling sick. He had a sudden memory of an elfin ten-year-old girl, violin case tucked under her arm, running for the school bus, flaxen hair flying. So long ago . . . so many lifetimes ago.

"It's your turn to give me something, Ben." She paused, relishing his torment. "Something you're very good at." A slight shifting, a tensing of muscles on the bare arm. "And this time you can't go running home to *Mama*." She spat out the last word with a little snarl.

Helene was shuddering now, shoulders and chest heaving. Her face had turned to chalk. But there were no tears in the green eyes, only a deep, bottomless hatred.

Tony yanked the long wooden handle, its scummy plunger rippling through water and sodden paper. Another jammed toilet. The fourth floor restroom by the elevator was always plugged up. In fourteen months Tony had found enough stuff in the drains to fill a boxcar. Today's prize was a slimy rubber lizard none the worse for its night in the toilet trap. He washed his hands and paged Danny.

"Restroom Twelve needs a Godzilla scrub. I'm due on the second floor."

Man, he was way behind schedule. They'd hollered about that leaky faucet in the Operating Room complex all evening, but going near the surgical center always freaked him out. He'd do the other jobs first.

Tony bolted from the rest room and threw out his hand to punch an elevator button. He tapped a rhythmic beat on the cool walls as he waited.

Two metal doors sighed open and Tony stepped lightly into the steel chamber, fingers snapping to the song in his head. Inside, two nurses from Maternity chatted quietly, heads bent. They stopped abruptly, staring blankly as Tony entered. He repressed a giggle, still tapping on the metal frame, then hopped out at the second floor and checked his work order: "Room 205 — bad light."

Second floor. Doctors' offices and more doctors' offices. *Hey. Cool babe coming out of Quaid's office!* Ten more doors — turn right. There shouldn't be anyone in this end of the building, but he rapped softly at Medical Records, 205.

No answer. He could hear the tap tap tap of spike heels receding behind him. Tony whipped out his keys and opened 205 as the elevator wheezed softly in the distance. The Records door clicked open to a cavernous room of faintly humming fluorescent lights, low-walled cubicles and banks of file cabinets.

Callie Martin's desk was a litter bomb of sticky notes, stubby pencils and Medicare forms. Dora Mayfield's work area was swept clean of every sign of human habitation except for a computer and one frantically blooming cactus which had gotten its seasons mixed up. Taweeka Johnson's cubicle had so many picture frames there was barely any work space.

Tony moved the chair away from Callie's desk and began stacking papers. *Man, I hope she doesn't see what I've done to her stuff!* His eye caught a lab report and Tony scanned briefly: "Cesarean. Surgeon: Benjamin T. Quaid." He shuddered. No blood for me, thanks.

A sputtering fluorescent bulb directly above Callie's desk signaled a bad ballast. Tony slid forms and note-pads to one side, then balanced on a metal chair. Quickly he shifted his weight to the desk and squeezed the plastic lens and ballast cover away from the fixture. A confetti of wingless flies and dead moths floated onto the jumble of papers. Tony replaced the ballast with a spare in his tool bag, then snapped the cover back in place.

He stepped nimbly to the floor and punched his maintenance radio. "Danny! Wanna sweep up some dead bodies in Records? Yeah. Bugs. Bring the vacuum." Maybe Danny would come, maybe not. Tony had no jurisdiction over the part-time janitor-come-lately.

Midnight. Time for serious calories. He'd had nothing since the bagel he'd stuffed in his face on the way to work. His stomach talked back big time.

Maybe Beth and Randy could grab a quick bite. He'd go upstairs and check. Punch Fourth Floor — Maternity. Silently the steel doors opened and Tony stepped in.

Outside the Nursery he paused in front of the newborns and studied their comic wrinkled faces. Every few days he picked a favorite and imagined the little mite recognized him as he tapped on the window.

8

Behind the glass, Beth Lansink twisted her sandy hair behind one ear and gave Tony a thumbs up. She pointed excitedly to the bassinet on her left. Front and center was the name: "Jimson." An olive-brown face peeked from under a white stocking cap, the tiny lips making little sucking movements. The baby stared solemnly, her breath coming quickly, the alert black eyes wide. Tony beamed with relief as he studied the tiny face. It was browning up, losing the sickly jaundiced hue.

He tapped the nursery window softly.

"Hey little girl. Hey Shana, Uncle Tony's here." Suddenly the peaceful face contorted, the mouth working furiously. A slow deep purple spread over Shana's cheeks as she let out a series of squalls. Like dominoes, every baby in the nursery joined a chorus of angry wails.

Tony laughed. *Lunchtime for babies too.* He pointed to Beth, then to his watch. "Five," Beth gestured, and Tony hunkered down on the carpet, leaning against the cool painted cinder blocks.

Once settled into his nightly routine, Tony resigned himself to the subdued pace of Shannon Memorial's night shift. Nurses conferred in hushed tones, doctors checked on a few troubled patients. Often the only noise was the wet swish of mops behind locked doors in the OR complex, punctuated by softly clanking buckets as the cleaning crew readied the big hospital for another crisis-filled day.

Tony straightened a little and watched Chief of Obstetrics Benjamin Quaid shuffle down the hall, shoulders stooped, eyes to the floor. One arm hung limply at his side, the other hand clutched a clipboard. He walked past one of the rooms, then stopped, looked at his clipboard and stared ahead blankly for several moments. Tony watched as the doctor turned, then disappeared into Room 412. *Emergency? Why's he still here at midnight?*

One of the nurses he'd seen in the elevator sat at her station, auburn hair caught up in a ponytail under a tiny cap. Her head was bent over a group of charts and her mouth moved silently as she

9

read. Loralee Otten was thirty-something. By-the-book. No nonsense, no smiles.

Tony saw the cleaning crew exit the OR one at a time, heading for the locker room to change clothes. Same thing every night. Tony could set his clock by the rhythms of Shannon Memorial. Slosh, slosh. Click click. Babies wailing. Doctors prowling.

And here was Tony, wondering if he'd be here for the rest of his life. He sighed as he joined Beth and headed for the cafeteria.

Beth hollered across the dining room. "Hey, Grab me a yogurt!" Tony snagged a carton of vanilla, then threw another sandwich on his tray. Beth was sure to want more.

"Man, I'm going broke buying stuff here." Beth's big frame slid into the booth next to Randy Dupree. "Maybe I should start bringing lunch."

Randy punched her arm. "Yeah. You could save a heap if you didn't pump iron, jog ten miles a day and try to beat me up every weekend."

Beth flushed. "A little bitty arm wrestle and you can't take it." She laughed and threw a french fry at his head.

Tony studied his friends across the table. Beth Lansink — good with babies and a terror on the athletic field. Randy Dupree — until last year the only male surgical nurse at Shannon Memorial. Now he was simply a second shift Registered Nurse, no longer working the OR. Tony didn't know what had prompted the switch, and he was not about to ask.

For over a year the threesome had shared lunch, a few laughs, and an occasional Saturday game of basketball or soccer. Did Randy and Beth have something going? He smirked, remembering the time Beth had arm-wrestled him to the table. She was a big girl — well-muscled and lithe as a cougar. Tony was short and wiry — like his little Spanish Mamita.

"Hey, you two! My potato's losing blood fast! Gimme a transfusion of ketchup over here!" Tony whacked the bottle and a blop of crimson covered his bun, cole slaw and baked potato. "Woo! How 'bout that! Looks like it's *dyin'* — okay, move along folks — we've got everything under control here!" Tony glanced quickly at Randy and Beth — they always picked up the routine.

Randy stared at his sandwich, slowly tracing lines on the crust. Beth shot him a brief glance, alarm and sympathy clouding her eyes.

"Whatsa matter, guys! Never seen a dead potato?" But Tony quickly choked off his next words. Randy looked straight past him — jaws clenched in a gray face.

"Gotta go." Slowly and very neatly Randy lined up his fork and knife on the cool steel table, then pulled back his chair. He stopped and turned to Beth. "You can have my sandwich."

Tony let the ketchup bottle slip from his hand. "What'd I say?"

Beth stopped in mid-chew and watched Randy shuffle out of the lunch room. "I dunno. He was really weird when I saw him an hour ago. Laughed one minute, clammed up the next." She shrugged. "But hey, I'm not gonna drag it outa him!"

With a practiced flick, Beth palmed Randy's sandwich and methodically began working her way through it.

––––––––––

At 4:55 a.m. Tony emerged from the basement door exhausted and dirty. He walked head down, hunch-shouldered, to the ghostly gray parking lot. His white Jeep glowed softly under a tall street lamp. Fifty yards away a Mazda hatchback, its windows open, sat partially hidden under a tree. Tony's Reeboks padded quietly, one untied shoelace tapping lightly on the asphalt.

A faint pink glow tinged the eastern sky, while a sleepy robin warbled a weak morning call.

Tony had one bright thought — maybe Dad was awake. Maybe he'd cook one of his famous scorched salsa omelets and they'd have breakfast before the six-thirty shift at the police station. Maybe. And maybe the apartment would be dead quiet and he'd fall exhausted on the bed and not see Dad again — and start another night fixing other people's broken things. Maybe.

"God only knows," he whispered.

But he didn't believe it.

He turned the key and the little buggy purred to life. The metal door thunked into place and Tony steered his Jeep quietly onto College Avenue, where it picked up speed and slipped like a phantom beneath tall sentinel lampposts and a dozen blinking traffic lights.

Tony fiddled with the stereo, got bleeps, fizzles and pops, then gave it up. Drumming his fingers on the steering wheel, he absently hummed a few bars to a country western.

The drive home should be his best time of the day. No more work for sixteen hours, and sunny daylight ready to explode into the world. But lately it had been his worst time. Lately he'd begun arguing endlessly with himself about his job, his empty love life and his future.

Sure, he could fix stuff. His shop teacher was always telling him he had "great potential," whatever that was. So how come he couldn't even land a decent job by himself? His father had pulled strings when the night maintenance guy was laid up last summer, and here he was, just keeping the pace, numbing his mind and hoping for better times.

Twenty minutes later he pulled into the apartment driveway next to his father's black GMC pickup and turned off the motor. He sat for a moment savoring the cool breeze of early morning.

A shrill whistle knifed through the quiet dawn. It started gently in a low key and rocketed sharply several notes higher before dropping back again. Then silence.

Dad! Tony stepped from the car, a wry smile working its way across his face. He trotted around to the grassy slope and caught the first faint whiff of eggs, tomatoes and onions.

By the time he reached the first deck landing, a hot-salsa fragrance was pulling him like a magnet. In three bounds he was up the stairs, unlatching the wide screen door. "Hey, Dad. They'll haul you in for disturbing the peace with that whistle."

"Hey yourself, Son. Don't just stand there. Grab a fork and fire extinguisher! This is the best yet. Guaranteed to lay you out flat!"

Jack Kowalski brushed a hand over his military-style salt and pepper hair. At fifty-two he was trim, muscular and just a bit over six feet. He eyed Tony with a grin and motioned towards the sink. "You're a good candidate for soap and water!"

Tony gave himself a quick splash under the faucet and whipped his hands through a towel.

"Been making mud pies?" Jack moved strong hands briefly over the back of Tony's neck, giving it a quick tight squeeze.

"I wish. Be a lot easier than fixing toilets." Tony plopped down at the table and plowed into the savory eggs.

"Hey! Careful with that chow. That's Grade-A stuff. Took me fifteen minutes." Jack grinned and moved the platter closer to Tony. "Eat up, Son."

"*Man*, that's hot!" Tony's eyes watered. He spluttered and chugged a tumbler of milk, then downed a second glass. He sat breathing hard, and soon began to hiccup.

"Watch it. I'll have to send you back to the hospital!" Jack enjoyed a short laugh, then laid a hand on Tony's shoulder. "Gotta go. Sorry. They want me at the precinct early. I think something's going down."

He reached for the door. "Oh. There's a message for you. Someone named Beth. . . ? Gotta go." He winked.

"Okay, Dad." Tony gulped down another huge mouthful. "I'm going early to Jimmy's before work tonight. So I might not see you 'til Thursday — unless we're both here this afternoon."

Jack raised an eyebrow, then grabbed his billfold and keys.

"Maybe. I'm not sure. Okay, Son. See you when I see you!" He smiled a quick goodbye and closed the door.

Jack had made a pact with Tony after high school graduation last year — his son's life and choices were now the sole property of Antonio Kowalski. But Tony's trips to Jimmy's always stretched Jack's patience. Jimmy Manelli did a lot more than run a pool hall, as everyone at the Cedar Bend Police Department knew.

Tony worked on the eggs another five minutes, mopping them up with buttered toast. He rinsed the dishes, then slid open the patio door and the screen. He grabbed a pillow off the sofa and molded it under his head, breathing deeply of the early morning coolness. He stretched his weary frame on the carpet, and in two minutes was deeply into a restless sleep.

As the sun knifed through the open door, Tony burrowed into his pillow and tensed his arms. And just as he had so many nights, he saw it again. The wide noisy street filled with diesel-spewing buses and trucks. His mother's shimmering black hair rippling in the breeze. Dad's intense, hurried walk. "C'mon, Son. Hurry. We're late." Tony tripping over his loose sandal . . . wrenching his hand from Mamita. The long, agonizing slow motion as Mamita knelt beside Tony. And the big gray truck.

Always the truck.

Closer, closer, its ugly grille and greasy tires gobbling up the road. His mother turning, pushing Tony. . . . Dad, running as if under water . . . mouth open in a frenzy of horror . . . the black wheels locked in a hellish squealing and skidding. . . .

Then a vacuum of silence. And once more Mamita floating like a rag doll — a blur of pink and white against the sky — falling, falling. . . .

A sickening thump as she hit the pavement.

"Mamita, Mamita!" Tony screamed as he had so many times

before. But Mamita could not hear, her limp body curled in an eternity of sleep, bright red blood trickling beneath her hair.

Tony woke gasping and sobbing. He felt the intense morning heat from the open doorway as flies buzzed around his head. He licked his parched lips and for several long minutes he sat with his head buried in the pillow, moaning. "You came back for me. You shouldn't have come. You shouldn't have come. My fault . . . . It was *my* fault."

Then he heard the latch turn, and his father's angry voice. "Tony! Good grief, close that door! Flies all over the place!" Tony's head throbbed. He pulled himself up from the hot carpet, closed the door and the drapes, then padded into the kitchen and flipped on the air conditioner.

"Sorry, Dad."

"Okay, okay. Didn't mean to bite you. Things didn't go well this morning. Missed our bust. Someone tipped them off." He snorted. "Oh well. We probably won't be in at the finish line anyway. Something about imports and drugs, and that means Customs, Immigration, Narcotics and a whole mess of agencies all trying to figure out who's boss. I have to go right back. Just stopped home for lunch."

Tony held his breath for the end of the story that never came. One or two sentences about Dad's police work was max.

"I thought you'd be gone. What's on your menu for the rest of the day, Son?"

"Maybe get my stereo fixed. Or get a new one." Tony scratched his neck and yawned. "It's flaking out on me. MegaBarn's having a sale. Then maybe fix Beth's carburetor. I dunno. Guess I'll have supper at her place."

"Well, I'm exhausted. Think I'll shower before heading back to work." Jack paused at the mantel and cast a longing look at the little black and white photo of Angelina, then disappeared into the bathroom.

Tony heard the muffled surge of water, then the musical scrape of curtain rings on metal. *Like ships passing in the night . . . that's us.* Tony brandished a swatter and spent the next ten minutes racking up tiny bodies on the floor. With a broom he gathered a fluffy mound of flies and dropped them in the trash. After a quick scrub in the kitchen sink, he slipped into shorts and tank top, grabbed a chunk of cold pizza and a soda, and bolted for his Jeep.

Marianna buttoned her blouse carefully. Twenty-two tiny button-holes. It was important to get them all closed, all the way to her chin. Great-Grandmother's blouse. She wanted to wear it tonight.

She slipped one arm into a sleeve. How gracefully her wrist flowed into her hand, she thought — like the precious Michelangelo in the Sistine Chapel. The cool musty nave had been a refuge last year — and with it the only season of peace she had ever shared with her mother. Marianna's eyes had been drawn to the painting of Mary's newborn. His face glowed, pulling golds and pinks from every crack in the nave. The curly little head, the trusting face — Marianna had wanted to touch him.

She tried to fasten the lower buttons, then gave it up and floated a large, shapeless tunic over her body. She pulled her shimmery-straight hair into a slow, severe twist, but released it suddenly and let it float to her shoulders. Her hair and oval face were flaxen pale.

Marianna reached slowly for lip gloss, then paused. No. No makeup. Not today. Today, she was what she was. Just Marianna. She slipped into black sandals and tiptoed down the hallway.

Don't wake Mother. Just leave.

———————

Jake squirmed. He felt the pressure of the seat belt and the hum of the Mazda. But where were the other sounds? Something was wrong. This was his special time with Marianna. He wondered why she didn't sing his favorite songs and laugh out loud in the middle and say, "Let's just make this one up." She always sang in the car, tapping her hand against the steering wheel. And sometimes she'd give Jake a quick pat and call him Little Bits.

The silence was a large presence. *Where are we going, Mama?*

Pressed close to his mother's side, Jake felt her tense body and the faint hum of the motor. The quietness grew and grew until it was a menacing intruder. Jake shrank within himself and groped for the only comfort he had — he sucked his thumb and went to sleep.

Ten p.m. Tony stretched his shoulders. His shift was half over. *Gotta fix that plumbing.* From the lobby, then up to Maternity to grab Beth for a snack date, then down to the boiler room to get his tools. *Just get it over with!* At the second floor the elevator coasted to a stop and the metal doors rumbled open.

A young girl walked to the center of the doorway, looked around wildly, then moved a couple of steps into the steel chamber. Tony noted the long hair like spider threads — some of them whipped across her mouth. She was wearing a long black coat. Too hot for a night like this.

"Going down?" Tony asked.

"Oh! No . . . I . . . guess not. . . . I just. . . . I'm. . . . I need . . . to . . . to see Dr. Quaid."

"Straight down that hall." Tony gestured with his thumb.

She glanced suddenly over her shoulder and backed out of the elevator. Tony watched her retreat, then continue down the hall. *Dr. Quaid? Office hours in the middle of the night?*

A final soft thump as the elevator reached the bottom of the hospital. Tony relished the peace of the boiler room and all the other cubby holes in this underground labyrinth. Maybe he could find something else to do down here and skip the operating rooms altogether. He felt weird just saying the words. He didn't know which label grossed him out more: "Operating Room" or just "The OR."

At 1:07 a.m. Benjamin Quaid finished checking a patient, then slipped out of Room 404. Beth saw him shuffle down the hall, head bent. She wondered why he was in the building so late.

Loralee Otten spotted Dr. Quaid and repositioned her stiff little hat. She stretched her mouth into a smile and slipped her tiny feet under the desk. "Yes, Doctor. The next surgery is eight a.m. Yes, sir. You are still scheduled in that slot."

"Well, I'm going to grab my gear and head for home. Eight o'clock will come early enough."

Quaid turned and walked back the way he'd come, then continued towards the OR. He turned, scanning the hallway outside the locker room.

No one.

He pushed open the wooden door with its little glass window and checked again.

Empty.

Mechanically he did what he'd been doing for twenty years in this hospital. He took off his shirt and pants, donned fresh scrubs, and popped an elastic paper bonnet onto his head. Then he sat on the short wooden bench and slipped paper boots over his shoes.

He opened the men's locker room door and checked the hallway. No one in sight. He walked a few feet and pressed five numbers on a walled key pad. The wide security doors of the OR fanned open and Doctor Benjamin Quaid again searched the hall, then slipped into the cold, brightly lit supply room of the Fourth Floor Surgical Complex.

The massive doors closed silently behind him. For a moment he was startled by the lights, beaming their unforgiving fluorescence on sterile surroundings. He moved towards the middle of the room, and across a little hallway he could see a light in one of the surgery rooms.

He looked through the window. Good. There was Randy Dupree, right on schedule.

Outfitted in mask and scrubs, Randy glowered at Quaid, then pulled the ribbon on the cloth instrument container, letting it fall in drapes over the Mayo stand. Without touching them he took mental inventory of the steel utensils, noting carefully the ones that would cut, clamp and cauterize. He covered them with a sterile sheet.

On the operating table a small gowned patient lay with her head behind a vertical blue drape, her upper legs made fast to the bed with a safety strap. Spiraling out from three patches on her chest and back were three wires connected to the EKG unit. A blood pressure cuff encircled one arm; an IV was inserted into the other. A hot blanket lay across her lower legs — a thin shield against the cold, sterile room.

Checking the anesthesia meds and equipment was a woman Quaid wished he'd never met. Penny Allen's gravely voice raked across the room, ripping through the double doors. "Okay, Honey. I'm just going to put this sticky pad on your upper leg. No, don't move. It won't hurt."

Deftly she took the cold wire protruding from the pad and plugged it into a Bovie on the side of the anesthesia machine. "Gotta get you grounded, Sweet Pea."

Quaid exhaled a long slow breath, then turned to the deep sink in the hallway. He pulled down a scrub packet from the wall shelf, tore it open and placed his knee against the faucet regulator.

Five minutes. He needed to scrub his hands and arms five minutes for his first surgery of the day. He bent over the sink and pried the little plastic pick under and around all ten of his manicured nails.

He soaped his hands again and again. He paid special attention to each finger in turn — those skilled, practiced fingers devoted to the saving of life.

Tiny bubbles refracted the light and for a moment Quaid stared at them in fascination. Then he pressed the tiny surgical cleansing brush against his short nails and shoved it back and forth savagely. He soaped again.

He knew he should not run the water so hot. It was nearly scalding his arms and hands. But somehow the pain comforted him, like payment on an old debt.

Quaid heard the double doors to his left whoosh with a gentle sigh, but kept his eyes lowered as Randy joined him at the double sink.

Silently they washed side by side. Then Quaid spoke: "I don't want any slip-ups."

Randy turned slowly, then continued washing.

Quaid: "We don't have the crematorium unit downstairs anymore."

Sounds of water . . . washing . . . more water.

Quaid mumbled, almost to himself. "Remember, you're supposed to meet. . . ."

"I *know*! Don't you think I know that?! Haven't you already told me a dozen times!?" Randy jerked his knee away from the faucet regulator. With a flick of his wrist he turned and backed into the surgery, arms pointed towards the ceiling.

Quaid could almost count the seconds of silence as Randy toweled dry, then the faint "snap-snap" of latex gloves.

The operating room was icy cold, but Randy Dupree sweated heavily under his scrubs and gown. Perspiration ran in rivulets down his sides and neck. He could use a comforting pair of hands right now, to wipe his clammy forehead. How in the world could one doctor and one nurse perform major surgery without help?

And why of all people did Quaid enlist Penny Allen, a nurse

anesthetist from the First Floor Operating Room? Everyone knew she had a big mouth. But Randy was beyond trying to puzzle through this nightmare of secrecy.

Why hadn't he said "no" before it was too late? *So all right, let Quaid blab all over the hospital about my little indiscretion last year. It ain't worth this to shut me up.*

Quaid could hear Penny's abrasive twang in the next room: "Just count backwards from a hundred, Sweetie. Ninety-nine, ninety-eight. . . . That's good. I can't hear you. Ninety-seven, ninety-six." Suddenly Penny's gutteral bark split the quiet — "She's intubated, Doctor!"

Quaid scowled as he entered the operating room, wet arms held high. "Move it, Dupree!"

Quaid squared his shoulders. Randy stood by the tray of sterile instruments, his jaw clenched, gloved hands poised over the gleaming steel.

Quaid held out a thumb and two fingers, and Randy put the precision-honed "skin" knife into the surgeon's open hand. Randy's eyes darted around the room — sweat was pouring off his forehead now, collecting in little puddles inside his mask. But he stood rock still, in the position he'd learned in nursing school, with hands folded over his stomach — waiting for the next command.

Penny stepped from behind the patient's head and roughly wiped Randy's brow, clucking her disapproval.

Dr. Quaid seemed to note for the first time that there was someone on the table. There was the brown-stained abdomen surrounded by prep sheets. The Betadine had done its job, dribbling off the surgical area in random streams. He blinked rapidly and stared as in a dream at his right hand — it was squeezing the blade handle in a death grip. He stood for one long moment and breathed heavily into his mask.

Randy shot a wild look at Quaid, then swiveled quickly to implore the anesthetist. Penny paused with her hand on the blue oxygen bag. She frowned with a tiny shake of her head, then slowly closed and opened both eyes and nodded her head.

With a sudden intake of breath, Dr. Quaid lifted the knife.

Jake had just drifted into a light sleep when he felt the first icy draft on his head. He curled his legs tighter and tried to pull away. But there was no room to move, and somehow he could not make his arms and legs work. More cold, and then more, until only his toes were still in the warmth of his bed. Hard slippery hands squeezed his legs against his chest and lifted him into a cruel coldness, moving him through a bigness of space that was never-ending.

A thump and a wave of air, then a hissing snarl and gasping breath . . . clanking metal . . . warm liquid trickling against his chest, his back, his head . . . a roughness and a constant rubbing . . . painful blue light . . . cold spears pressing into his nose, sucking against the inside of his head. Jake gagged.

Helene Morrow lay as still as stone against her satin pillows, eyes fixed on the antique silver clock near her bed. One fifty-five. Doctor Benjamin Quaid's job was done.

With her left hand she began to move her thumb slowly back and forth across a tiny piece of stained fabric. Over and over she caressed the cotton nubs, worn thin and limp over the years. Hot tears poured against the clenched jaws from narrowed green eyes.

It was not so very sweet after all. . . .

Rats. Only an hour til the end of his shift. No more excuses. He'd have to fix that leaky faucet in the Fourth Floor Operating Room complex.

The dreaded OR.

Tony sighed. "Here I go on the prowl again."

Up the elevator, down the hall.

The fourth floor was ghostly quiet. Even Nurse Otten was gone from her station. Computer monitors glimmered softly at the main desk, where one of the nurses sat in the far corner with her back to the hall, intent on the glowing screen.

Tony moved past the silent nursery and paused. There was Beth hovering over a bassinet. He walked to the end of the hall near the OR, pushed the code buttons on the wall, then stepped through the security doors. It was always cool, nearly cold, in this part of the hospital. Hard waves of icy air tingled his face and gave him fresh energy.

He moved quickly through the supply room, turned left, then walked a few short steps through a small storage area that looked like a kitchenette. Sure enough, water was dribbling in a slow stream from the faucet.

Quickly he opened his tool box and laid out wrench, rubber washer and screwdriver. Then he cranked the cutoff valve beneath the sink. In a few short minutes Tony had the faucet apart.

He was about to insert a new washer when he heard a muted squeaking. He paused, frowning, and glanced around. A new maintenance problem at this late hour wasn't in his game plan.

There it was again. He wheeled and noticed a half-open door at right angles to the kitchenette. He moved towards the entrance and felt waves of heat pulsing from the interior. He prodded the door a little wider and hesitated.

Inside the dimly lit room, motors hummed. Gauges and wires and pipes abounded in wild confusion. A steel cart blocked his way so he shoved it aside.

He'd been in this room before, and because he was precise in his work he was a little ticked that it didn't have a name, or even a number. "Oh, we just call it 'the back-of-the-autoclave' room," was the response from most nurses.

Two giant sterilizing autoclaves could be opened from the supply room, but their bulging tank-like structures extended into this special chamber.

The entire room hummed with suppressed energy. Those steam-powered autoclaves could top eight hundred degrees in their well-insulated interiors, an aggressive heat that was hard to tame. In this little room Tony figured it must be well over ninety. He was already sweating.

He started backing out of the room, then paused. One of the autoclaves, or maybe one of the pipes, emitted a shrill, high-pitched whine. He knelt first beside Autoclave One, then Autoclave Two, trying to locate the trouble. But it was nearly impossible with the persistent thrumming of motors.

There it was again, only this time it was more of a squeak. Now that he thought about it, the noise wasn't coming from the autoclaves or the pipes.

Tony quickly turned his head from side to side, trying to isolate the sound. He checked the radio on his belt, then switched it off. He moved past the cart and walked to the entrance of the room. He stood without breathing.

There it was again, louder. And there was no mistaking that sound now. He'd heard it many times before. It was a baby crying.

What. . . ? Tony retreated into the kitchenette, then a few steps farther into the main supply area, and waited. Surely there couldn't be a C-section in one of those operating rooms. He'd checked with the nurses, checked the schedule. There wasn't supposed to be anyone in here at all, and he'd seen no activity in the vacant outer rooms.

Then he heard it again. But this time it was coming from behind him. He moved cautiously back toward the autoclave room — and the sound, though muffled, was louder. The rippling wail was jagged and shuddery.

Tony looked around wildly, then bumped the surgical cart. Near the bottom, a deep lower drawer was open a few inches. Carefully he gave it a tug, and a movement in the shadowy interior caught his eye.

Little bulges appeared and disappeared under a thin piece of cloth. Suddenly a doll-sized arm poked out from the fabric. Tony gasped, nearly falling back against the wall. He reached out a tentative hand and opened the drawer all the way.

A tiny baby lay wrapped in a discarded surgical gown, nestled on a bed of bunched towels. Its head and arms, the color of warm honey, were covered with reddish-brown streaks. Dried blood matted the little fuzz of hair. Instinctively Tony reached out a greasy finger and laid it on the tiny hand. The baby clutched it with a strong grip and continued wailing.

Hey, Man. How in the world.

Tony gently pulled away his finger, then closed the drawer halfway. "Don't cry, Kid. okay?" He scanned the hallway quickly. No one. Then he stepped outside the autoclave room and locked the door. His first thought was to holler at Nurse Otten. But a deep wariness learned from his father made him pause.

Beth. She'll know what to do.

Man!

Two nurses sat feeding their little stocking-capped babies behind the glass window. Beth finally noticed a movement in the hall and raised a questioning eyebrow. Tony frowned and yanked his thumb towards the door. Beth nodded and held up two fingers.

Tony gave a quick nod and began pacing. Suddenly there was movement outside Room 405. Nurse Otten emerged, then marched towards the desk without turning her head. Tony's heart pounded.

Another minute and Beth came out giggling. "Boy, you're a mess. Whatcha been doing, playing in the dirt?"

Tony grabbed her arm and steered her down the hall with tense whispers. "C'mere. No, don't talk. Just hurry!"

"Hey! What're. . . ."

"Just shut up. Trust me." Tony clutched Beth's arm in a painful grip.

"Wait! Get back!" Tony paused, head down, pretending interest in his radio, stealing glances towards the main desk. Nurse Otten noted the grimy coveralls and gave Tony a cast-iron frown. She spoke to one of the nurses and looked back at him again. She stood uncertainly for a moment, then turned and walked around the corner of the horseshoe hallway. Tony exhaled slowly.

"S-s-s-t!" Tony motioned for Beth, then steered her through the double doors and down the hall, into the OR complex. By now he was sure they'd completely messed up the sterile environment of the whole area, but he'd worry about that later.

They were just rounding the corner towards the kitchenette when they heard a muted "ping" like metal hitting metal.

"Sh-h-h! Back here!" Tony pushed Beth behind a set of shelves where they stood breathing heavily.

"I don't know what that was," Tony whispered. "There's not supposed to be anyone in here!" Quietly the two of them tiptoed the extra few feet towards the autoclave closet — then Tony unlocked the door and jerked Beth inside.

"Look, you'd better. . . ."

"Quiet!" Tony let go of Beth's arm and closed the door.

"*Please*. . . . Please be quiet." His voice softened. "Just look."

He turned to the cart and pulled it into the middle of the room. "Pull that drawer all the way open."

Beth tugged on the handle and caught her breath in a gasp. Both hands flew to her mouth. "Oh, Tony! Where did you. . . . How. . . ?"

"Look, I don't know who put that baby here. But it's alive. I think it's a newborn!"

"Let me look." Beth was all business, unwrapping the rumpled gown, gently peeling it back from the sticky blood.

"Tony, See this? The umbilical cord still has a clamp on it. Just look at him! He's probably no more than five pounds. He's a preemie. Tony, this little guy needs attention big time. This is horrible — I've got to tell someone. . . . It's. . . ."

"You're not going to tell anyone." A low, icy command came from the open doorway. Randy Dupree moved in quietly, turning the lock behind him.

Randy slumped to the floor and leaned heavily against the grimy wall. "Hand me the baby."

Tony picked up the little infant and the towels, then set the whole bundle on Randy's lap. Beth just stared and for once had nothing to say. Randy pulled a small nursing bottle and a fresh diaper from his lab coat pocket. "Get me a clean cloth. Wet it down."

Beth looked around the dim room. "Sure. Okay."

She moved towards the door, then stopped. "I can't. Tony's got the faucet all apart. Wait. I know. Here!" She pulled a tiny packet of baby wipes from her jacket. Deftly she cleaned off the blood while the baby pulled tentatively on the nipple, his little mouth working courageously — his cheeks fluttering in and out. The honey-brown face wrinkled in concentration. All three watched intently as the drama unfolded. This was the tiny infant's first meal — and they each hoped it would not be his last.

Beth was the first to speak. "What's going *on!*"

Randy sat frowning, jaws clamped. Against the humming of the autoclaves, sounds never heard in this room mixed in strange concert. Randy's heavy breathing blended with the baby's little splutters.

Slowly, Randy's deep breaths became irregular as he struggled for control. Then his face crumpled and his shoulders began to shake violently. He gasped once, then began a long, soundless sobbing. He covered his face first with one hand — then with the other.

Tony grabbed the blanketed infant and the bottle as Beth moved over to wrap Randy in her wide arms. "Randy, Randy. Ssh-h-h. Sh-h-h. Don't, don't, Honey. It's okay, it's okay."

For long moments there was just the quiet sobbing and the little sucking sounds. Tony stared at the baby, fascinated with the tenacious strength of the tiny body. The little eyes seemed to follow his every movement.

"I've gotta . . . get him outa here," Randy whispered between sobs. "They'll . . . kill him. I know they will. Quaid, he told me . . . wanted me to. . . ." He stopped, his shoulders shaking convulsively. "It's. . . . You don't know them. . . . They're. . . ."

Suddenly Randy jerked upright, eyes wild with fear. "Give me the baby! I've gotta get him outa here — I have to hide him!"

"I'll take him." Tony pulled the baby towards his chest, feeling the warmth of its fragile body and the rapidly beating heart. He stared long and hard at Randy, and for several moments the four characters in the little drama were as still as statues. "My shift's over. I'll call in sick tomorrow."

Beth threw a warning look at Tony. "But your dad. . . . He's a *cop*!"

"Dad's cool. He'll help. I don't know how, but he'll help. We've got different shifts. It'll work." Tony's first impulse had taken root while Randy sobbed. The little babe had looked straight at him, had gripped his finger with a plea for help.

For several minutes the only sound in the autoclave room was the heavy thrumming of motors. Slowly Randy unfolded his legs and raised himself against the dingy wall. He looked down at the floor, then with a quick decisive nod and a last shuddering sob he raised himself against the wall and whipped into action.

"Look, don't tell me what you're going to do. I don't want to know. Just get outa here and don't let anyone see you. I'll leave first and distract the nurses. Beth, you get a bag of stuff for the baby."

Randy touched one finger lightly on the baby's little puff of black fuzz, and his lips quivered in a short smile.

"Tony. Watch your back, man."

5

Lightning flashed between black clouds as Tony opened the basement door a tiny crack. He took a quick scan of the lower driveway and adjusted his eyes to the gloom.

No one else around — at least that he could see in the early-morning darkness.

Cumulus clouds were rolling in fast, and Tony realized with a sick shock that he'd left the Jeep's canvas cover off.

"Let's hurry, Kid." Tony hefted the gym bag filled with his stow-away and sprinted up the service driveway to his Jeep.

He shifted the bag to his chest and mumbled into the zipper opening: "No poking outa your hiding place."

There was no answering sound. In Tony's left hand he clutched a bundle of rags. Hanging from one finger was a plastic bag with a jumble of diapers and a confusing array of tubes and bottles — all containing various consistencies of mystery goop.

There was just enough milk for twenty-four hours. And a packet of tiny shirts.

Beth had packed in a hurry.

Tony walked quickly to his car and carefully stowed his strange cargo onto the bundle of rags, sliding it gently under the dashboard. The Jeep purred out of the parking lot, onto the wide and empty College Avenue.

Two blocks from Tony's apartment the skies opened. Rain fell in undulating gray sheets, whipped by a rising wind. Frantic, Tony shoved the gym bag farther under the dash, then stopped to pull the zipper nearly closed.

By the time he'd reached home, most of the Jeep's contents were soaked. He grabbed a tarp from behind the seat and made a crude poncho for himself and his baggage, then bolted for the stairs.

It was a sodden menagerie that greeted Jack Kowalski in the kitchen.

"Leave the top at home again?" Jack grinned, then quickly sobered as he caught the frantic urgency in Tony's eyes.

"What's wrong?"

"Dad, please. . . . There isn't. . . . Grab me a towel." Tony gasped for breath and stripped off his wet shirt. Quickly he knelt and unzipped the bag. He dragged the blanketed stowaway onto the carpet and began toweling down the little fuzz-topped head. Then he rocked back on his heels and started drying his own hair. He gave his father a quick look from under the terrycloth.

"Tony, for God's sake! What are you doing with that kid? Whose is it?" Jack was frozen in place, his mouth open.

Tony searched his father's face. "I found this little guy in the autoclave room, covered with blood." His dark eyes snapped. "Randy Dupree's convinced somebody wants this baby dead. You know Randy's made of steel, Dad. But . . . you should have seen him. He was blubbering like a little kid."

Tony stopped for breath. "Dr. Quaid's mixed up in this but there's somebody else, and Randy's scared to death of him. . . . I just . . . I don't know . . . . It's really weird."

Jack knelt by the tiny bundle. "Tony, this is . . . this is *not* a mess you should get into. Please. Let me take him down to the Department. Now!"

"NO!" Tony's outburst was swift. "Dad, if this isn't a mess I should get into, then . . . who . . . whose is it?" Tony paused, breathing hard. "Randy and Beth can't count on their roommates. And if you take him to the station, how do you know the wrong person won't find him?" Tony clenched his jaw in frustration. "Randy says there's a City Hall dude mixed up in this."

He paused, straightening to his full height. "There *isn't* anybody else, Dad. If you and I don't take care of him he's a dead kid."

Jack Kowalski, twenty-six-year police veteran, was having a great deal of trouble digesting this new dilemma. He paced the floor, one hand massaging the back of his neck. Drugs, murder, burglary . . . yes, and child abuse. He'd seen it all. But a baby hidden in the hospital and brought home in a gym bag?

Jack stared for a moment at Tony's blazing eyes and decided to play for time. "Well, we can talk later. Right now, I think this kid needs some help."

Jack knelt on the floor for a long moment, staring at the child. His eyes softened. "He's so terribly small."

"Here's some stuff Beth gave me. Her shift's done in about an hour. Then she's coming over."

"Thank God for that. What does this baby eat?"

Tony opened the bag and brought out a nursing bottle with a plastic cap. "It's not regular formula. It's something special for preemies. Something like 'colos' or 'costos' — I can't remember. Anyway, he ate a little bit about an hour ago, so Beth says he'll probably sleep a couple more hours. Man, I could use some Z's too!"

As if on cue, the baby squirmed and scowled. Then his face turned mud-brown with some private agony. Neither Jack nor Tony were prepared for the sound that blasted from the little bundle. It began as mournful wailing, then escalated to steady jagged cries.

"Good *grief,* Kid!" By the time Tony picked him up, an angry siren was blasting from the tiny baby, his whole body shuddering and tight. "What'll I do, Dad? He couldn't be hungry."

"Maybe he's wet." Jack peeled back the diaper. "Uh oh. Look, here's the problem." Inside was a horror of blackish green stuff. Tony had never seen anything like it. He ran for the sink and retched.

Jack chuckled softly. "It'll get better. This stuff is what you call meconium."

"What's that?" Tony's head was still over the sink.

"It's what a newborn puts in his first diaper. Was he clean when Beth checked him?"

"Um yeah, I think so."

"Believe me, you'd know. I hope you've got some baby wipes in that bag."

"Wipes?"

"Should be a square plastic box. We'll need it to clean up this mess." Tony found the pop-up box, and Jack pulled out a handful of tough wet tissues. "This is the only demonstration you'll get, Son. When I'm not here, you're on your own."

Quickly he went through four wipes in a mega-cleaning job, slathering the baby with zinc ointment as a finishing touch. Tony held a napkin over his mouth and cautiously kept one hand on the sink. By the time Jack had fitted the tiny disposable diaper, the baby had stopped yowling and was hiccuping through muted sobs. Then he stared soberly at the two men, one little fist pushing into his cheek.

"There's that look again." Tony grinned, awed by the wise little face. "You're all right, Kid. You're *jake*," he said, mimicking his father's favorite slang. "Yeah, you're jake." He turned to his father. "Hey. That's what I'll call him — Jake!"

His father wasn't prepared for the sudden stinging behind his eyes. In her halting English, Angelina had once called him Jake.

He nodded curtly and ducked into the entryway. "I got this box in the mail yesterday. It's heavy and looks pretty clean. You can line it with towels."

He put his hand gently on Tony's shoulder. "Son, this will be the hardest thing you've ever done." He paused and sized up the baby and his surrogate father. "I've gotta go. I'll keep my ears open, see what I can dig up at the precinct."

At Tony's sudden frown, Jack opened his hands defensively. "Don't worry. I won't say anything. I'll just listen."

"Thanks, Dad . . . for everything. It's. . . . I wish Mamita. . . ."

"I know. . . . I know."

Jack turned quickly, grabbed his billfold and keys and opened the apartment door. Never in his wildest imaginings could he have thought Tony would show up this morning with a stowaway kid. Jack clicked the door shut and started down the hall.

How many hours could you keep a thing like this hidden? His mind scrolled down the possibilities. *Think of something, Jack. Do something!* He'd known plenty of judges in his time — faced with this weird scenario, all of them without exception would be thumbing through their code books deciding between Child Endangerment, Kidnapping, or Child Stealing. In those books they would *not* find a section on "Child: Rescue. Subsection B: Automatic Adoption by Teenage Father."

But at least, Jack thought wryly, he's not playing pool at Jimmy's.

Tony made a little bed for Jake, then awkwardly lifted him onto the makeshift cushion of towels. "I can't give you much, Kid. What you see is what you get." He laid his hand lightly on Jake's hand, and was rewarded with a touch from the tiny fingers. The two sized each other up for a moment, then the baby's eyelids grew heavy.

Jake had no idea where he was, but it was quiet and it was warm. It would do for now.

Tony collapsed on the sofa and slipped wearily into deep slumber. A half hour later he was jolted awake by the doorbell's harsh buzzing. Outside, Beth stood breathing hard, damp hair plastered to her head. "Where is he!" She pushed past Tony, squeezing him painfully against the door jamb.

Tony jerked a thumb over his shoulder and yawned. "Over there. In the box."

"In a BOX!!? You put him in a BOX!?" Beth rushed over to the cardboard container, rolling up her sleeves for action.

Tony scratched under his arms and rubbed his eyes, then eased back onto the sofa. "Yeah. I think he likes it. What — you didn't think I could keep a kid alive for a few hours?"

Beth studied the baby, gave Tony a sly look, then opened her mouth in a wide grin. She winked and punched his upper arm. "Hey, Daddy my man! He looks great!" She let out a huge sigh and plopped onto the sofa. Tony bounced up a couple of inches.

Beth folded her arms and lowered her voice to a moan. "I'm beat. Oh man, Tony, I keep hoping I'll wake up and find this was all a bad dream. I talked to Randy again. Quaid's in it up to his eyeballs, with some nurse-anesthetist named Penny. Somehow they managed to sneak into the OR, do a cesarean and drag the mother out the basement door of the hospital without anyone seeing them."

She frowned in concentration. "Quaid must have something on Randy. I've never known him to even think about doing something like this."

She paused, cracking her knuckles. "Randy's scared to death."

"Of Quaid? Nah. He's a teddy bear."

"Not just Quaid! It's higher up than that. . . . A lot higher up."

"Who?"

"I dunno. Randy knows just a little piece of this whole mess. But. . . ." Beth's eyes clouded.

"But what?"

"Well, what Randy *does* know is that these aren't the kind of guys who would just let us walk away with this baby. Tony . . . they'll come after all of us."

Beth and Tony sat side by side, each with their private nightmares.

Jake whimpered in his sleep.

"Do you . . . do you think this kid's gonna make it? I'm giving him everything I've got, but . . . maybe that's not gonna be enough. God only knows," he finished lamely.

Beth glanced over at the box. "Does he have a good pair of lungs on him?"

"Man, are you *kidding*? That little guy's got two tweeters and a woofer!"

"Good! Means he's not as bad off as I thought." Beth squared her shoulders. She leaned forward, all business. "We'll need lots of stuff. A crib. Some clothes. Thermometer. I can get some of this from Melanda Jimson. She. . . ."

"You mean Shana's mom? Your friend who just had the baby?"

"Yeah. Melanda could use the money, so we can buy her secondhand stuff. A couple of years ago she had twins, and now she's got double everything! Better yet, she can give us some milk." Beth was warming to her plan, moving around the room, gesturing widely.

"Milk. . . ."

"Yeah. As soon as this kid finishes the colostrum I sneaked out of the nursery, he's gonna need the real thing. He'll never make it with formula."

"But . . . wha. . . ."

Beth stopped and stared open-mouthed at Tony. "Oh, man — do I have to spell it out for you?"

Tony's face reddened. "I don't need a spelling lesson. Just do what you have to do and don't tell me about it."

Jake stretched and yawned, smacking his lips and puckering his face in little comic frowns. Suddenly, like shades popping up, his eyes opened.

"Well, here we go again." Beth leaped up. "I'll warm one of the bottles. Tony, You change his diaper."

She giggled to herself as she opened the fridge. "And when you're finished I'll walk you through Baby Care 101."

Tony sighed deeply. Man, it was going to be a long day.

6

Furman Adams waited under a willow tree by the river. A soft pink grayness behind the cattails and scrub bushes heralded the approaching sunrise.

He could hear water lazily lapping against the exposed tree roots and bare earth. A moist smell of decaying leaves hung on the quiet air.

Furman was out of place here, with his thousand-dollar Lucchese alligator boots and tailored Armani suit. He stepped forward to get a wider view of the river, and cursed softly when one boot sank into greenish ooze.

The faint purr of a motor brought his head up sharply, and he squinted into the pre-dawn haze. A small motorized craft suddenly materialized under the willow tree.

Furman's shoulders relaxed, but he made no move to help Jimmy Manelli tie up the boat. The two men assessed each other silently. Furman kept his eyes on Jimmy while he fingered a diamond ring on his manicured hand. "Well?"

Jimmy took his time securing the boat. He stepped on shore and wiped his hands on an oily cloth. He fixed Furman with worried eyes. "Job's not finished. The item in question wasn't where it was supposed to be."

"What do you mean?" Furman's eyes snapped.

"I dunno, but I think Quaid messed up. That nurse guy musta

sneaked it out of the hospital 'stead of stashin' it where Quaid told me."
There was a deathly pause while Jimmy tried to recover the advantage. "It could be dead — we don't know. And that could be okay." Jimmy attempted a smile, warming to his excuse. "You know things like that, they . . . they don't live long . . . and. . . ."

Furman's eyes narrowed to murderous slits.

Jimmy snorted uneasily. "Quaid's a fink. He can't control some dumb nurse kid."

"Now you listen to *me*!" Furman's dark hand snaked out suddenly and grabbed Jimmy by the front of his shirt. He lifted him until they were nose to nose. Jimmy smelled the stale cigar and tasted acid saliva as Furman spat out his threat. "If there's no dead *i-tem*," he snarled, "there won't be any more import deals. You got that? No. More. *Deals!*"

Jimmy gulped noisily and stepped back, eyes darting towards the river and back to Furman, who was mumbling obscenities and breathing heavily.

Slowly Furman's eyes raked contemptuously over Jimmy and he relaxed, his mouth twisting into a sneer. "You have three days, Manelli. Three days. And I don't do broken deals. Either you take care of that little item, or you're going to be missing more than an import deal. You're going to be missing your head."

Jimmy blanched. Furman's last few words had been spoken quietly and calmly. For a moment Jimmy was not sure he had heard correctly. Now he remembered what had been whispered about the mayor of Cedar Bend. There were no idle threats in Furman's deals, no negotiating, no extension of time.

Jimmy nodded, swallowed hard, then turned abruptly and got back into the boat. Yanking violently on the outboard motor's rope, Jimmy maneuvered the little craft out of the cove.

Jimmy Manelli now had one all-consuming focus. He would take care of that little "item" if it was the last thing he did.

A few wispy clouds scuttled across the sky while the spent storm growled in the distance. In the late morning gloom, the sprawling brick home glistened darkly. A couple of hundred yards down the road Carver Adams leaned against the fender of his Lexus and studied the vast rolling lawn, the formal flower garden and the towering glass atrium. He lit a cigarette and squinted through the smoke, trying to decide what to do.

Marianna had not called last night. Or the night before. Marianna's best friend did not know where she was. Or at least she was not telling Carver Adams. School had already begun, Cassie said, and Marianna had not shown up for the first day of classes.

At least twice a week for the last year Carver had received those late-night calls from Marianna, and sometimes they'd met secretly to plan their life together. Carver knew better than to be around when her mother was home. He had done that once before and he winced at the memory of her tightly-sprung malice.

Just to play it safe, a few minutes ago he had scoped out Morrow Imports. Helene's powder-blue Porsche had been parked behind the building.

But who owned the white custom van in front of Marianna's house? Carver moved in front of his car to get a better view. He noted the drawn curtains and the closed garage. Finally he made up his mind. Someone was in that house, he was sure. But even more sure was his need for Marianna.

Carver dropped the glowing stub onto the gravel and opened the car door. He settled into the supple leather cushions and slowly turned the key. The Lexus purred to life and crunched down the gravel road toward Marianna's house. As he pulled up the steep concrete driveway he thought he saw a curtain flutter.

Carver pulled close to the garage, where his car stayed hidden by the white van and a stiff row of stately evergreens. He sat gripping the steering wheel with wet palms.

Finally he took a deep breath, clicked open the door and stepped quietly onto the concrete. He straightened his shoulders and walked towards the back door. The sound of his own footsteps startled him and he froze for a moment, eyes to the ground.

Near the bottom of the deck's redwood stairs, a row of yellow and purple pansies turned their moist tired faces up to him. Slowly and fearfully he lifted his eyes again to the top of the porch. All was quiet. Too quiet.

The stairs and the wide wooden decking were stoutly built, so Carver was able to muffle his soft footfalls. Once he was across the planks to the right of the door he marshaled his courage and looked sideways into the window. Cautiously he brought his head around and peered directly into the massive kitchen and beyond it to the living area.

He could just barely see a television set flickering on the far side of the room, and perpendicular to this was a black leather sofa. He saw what looked like a frilly white fringe of hair resting on the leather arm. Carver waited.

The white head did not move. Carver lifted his hand to tap on the door, then hesitated. The door was open a few inches.

He pushed and it swung noiselessly into the kitchen. Carver moved inside and took a few hesitant steps. He came closer and closer to the white fringe of hair, his chest thumping painfully.

But still there was no movement. Carver came abreast of the sofa and heard a faint snuffle. A woman lay with her eyes closed and her mouth open. Crackling faintly on the table behind her was a white plastic device, its cord plugged into the wall. It emitted a faint wheezing noise. He waited one long, eternal minute, trying to control his breathing.

The regular little whiffling snores continued.

Carver turned left down a polished-oak hallway. He knew the way to Marianna's room. Once he had come here when she was supposed to be alone. That was the dreadful night they had been surprised by Helene.

On and on he walked, in quiet, regular steps. Carver's great fear was always that he would be caught — caught lying, caught failing, caught trying to be with the girl he loved.

At the far end of the hall Carver hesitated. He looked behind him. No sound. He stared at the blank white expanse of Marianna's closed door.

"Marianna!" His whisper was urgent. "Marianna!"

No sound.

Slowly he turned the handle and pushed.

Beyond the door the once-playful pink and white room had been transformed. The windows were draped heavily with sheets, and in the lavender-gray light a bank of monitors beeped and glowed behind a steel bed. Carver could see the soft outline of a slim body.

Three feet above the bed, a plastic tube swung in a graceful arc from a plump translucent bag. Somewhere on that body it connected.

Carver stood rooted to the floor. "Marianna?" His voice caught in a sob.

The girl on the bed slowly turned her head, following the sound of his voice. She looked towards Carver with dull eyes.

"Marianna . . . I'm . . . I'm here."

Silence.

"Marianna . . . what . . . what happened? What is this? You must tell me. . . ."

Marianna closed her eyes. She lay deathly still. "I must not . . . do anything."

Carver took a few hesitant steps.

"They took him . . . ." Marianna's voice was clear and faint, like tinkling ice. One hand fluttered to her face. "He's gone."

"Gone. . . ? Who. . . ?"

Marianna turned her head towards the window. Carver noted for the first time the flattened contour of her body. A slow dawning widened his eyes and contorted his mouth.

"No. . . ." Carver stood over the bed, moving his head slowly from side to side. "No . . . Marianna . . . *no.*"

He reached dark hands towards her frail body, tears splashing down his cheeks.

Benjamin Quaid trembled as he looked at the heavy coffee mug in front of him. THE BEST DAD IN THE WORLD was printed in orange block letters at the top. He brought the container to his lips and tried to drink. But there was his right hand again, shaking uncontrollably.

He steadied the mug with the long fingers of his left hand and grimaced.

On a plate in front of him, scrambled eggs and toast grew cold on a pale green plate. The refrigerator hummed softly while Marta poured a china pitcher of fresh coffee at the counter. She brought it to the table and eyed him steadily.

"What is it, Ben?" Slowly she pulled up a chair, sat down and waited. Over a tumultuous ten years she'd learned to be patient. Discovery took time. And so did forgiveness.

The refrigerator stopped humming. The silence in the kitchen was palpable, leaving space that neither Ben nor Marta wanted to fill. Ben reached out a hand and laid it on Marta's.

He turned dull eyes towards his wife. "I said I'd never hide anything from you again, Marta. But I was wrong. What I . . . I did . . . I. . . ." Ben's hands squeezed hard on the cup and he forced himself to gulp the strong black brew. He began to cough. Marta sat very still.

"Look at me, Marta." He lifted one hand and held it a few inches above the table, where it began shaking violently. Ben dropped it suddenly into his lap and bowed his head.

"I will tell you, Marta. I will. But . . . not yet. Not yet." His shoulders slumped as Ben faced his private agony in the mirror of dark liquid.

Marta and Ben sat side by side minute after slow minute, each hoping for escape, but powerless to make the first move. Then gradually Marta began sliding back her chair. She slipped from the room and walked with leaden steps towards the dark, cool basement — the place she'd always gone as a child to hide her private grief.

So this is how it would be again. Only this time, she did not think she could bear it.

Jack eased out of his pickup and leaned for a moment against the front fender. He took in the low-slung City Hall with its nineteen-sixties stark angles. He noted which windows glared darkly and which ones shone brightly in front of drawn shades. He noted the speed and the posture of his fellow police officers as they arrived for the six-thirty shift.

Decoding people's actions was a technique he'd picked up during his Texas Border Patrol days, and more than once it had saved his life.

By the time he'd descended the dim basement stairway, Jack Kowalski was already forming today's profile of the City Hall staff.

Police Chief Gordy Duncan had walked slowly, head bowed in thought. Mayor Furman Adams had marched angrily, one hand straightening and re-straightening a silver-blue tie, the other hand waving — or was it dismissing — attempts from his staff to wish him a good morning.

First-year rookie Lynn Fallows had nearly sprinted from her perky little Volkswagen into the building, chin held high. The newly hired investigator Ross Schade, who early had identified himself with "I don't drink coffee, thanks," was sheepishly polishing off a cup of Joe at the refreshment bar.

Jack greeted him with a thump on the shoulder. "What's with

the caffeine?"

Ross grimaced. "Couldn't sleep last night. But you're looking way too wide awake, man. We'll have to do something about that. What're you working on this week?"

"Still hammering on that investigation at Manelli's. DNE's as stumped as we are. And that's going some for those Narc guys. Why? Got something big?"

"Three break-ins at Regal Oaks. All last night."

Jack let out a low whistle. Regal Oaks was all manicured lawns and BMWs. "What's the report?"

"That's the weird part. Nothing missing but video tapes."

"We're not doing any good standing here. Let's roll."

Jack buckled his shoulder holster in place and turned for the door. "You driving?"

Ross sported a sleepy-eyed, wicked grin. "Yep."

Jack rolled his eyes. Ross was an aggressive driver, an Indy 500 wannabe in uniform. He was perpetually speeding, but ironically his favorite stress reliever was to slow to the speed limit and accumulate dozens of cars behind him — their drivers, lemming-like, suddenly obedient to the law.

Jack and Ross settled into the white Ford sedan and buckled up. Jack would spend the next two or three hours with this new guy, trying to get a fix on anything smelling like a domestic crisis.

It wouldn't take long to connect the dots and figure out where that fugitive baby came from. Investigator Jack Kowalski had an inborn radar that zoomed in on bits and pieces of conversation. And that's how he'd get to the bottom of the kidnapping or abandonment or whatever it was.

Jack wanted Tony as far away from this mess as he could get him, because Jack had learned years ago that where children were in crisis, nobody — not the family, not the police or judges, not the Department of Human Services — could be counted on to think straight.

Normally he would have trusted his fellow police officers with the facts that he saw unfolding around his son. But not today. Today he would listen with his border-patrol ears.

Jack assumed a casual manner and spun out a series of questions as they headed toward Regal Oaks. He fiddled with a bag of potato chips and glanced at Ross. "Hear about that missing kid in Salina, Kansas last month?" He ripped open the chips and started popping them in his mouth. "Missing for days. Just a baby. They found her in some guy's car."

"Yeah?" Ross yanked the sleek sedan onto Hubbard Avenue and gunned it. "How much time did he do?"

"It could go either way. He didn't steal the baby. She wound up in his back seat, but he wasn't the one who stole her."

Ross reached over and helped himself to chips. He shook his head slowly. "I hate those abuse cases. I dunno why women bring babies into the world if they're not gonna take care of 'em."

"We haven't had that many abuse cases this year." Jack turned his attention to the construction site on his right, flicking crumbs off his shirt.

"Nope. Thank God for that! I had a belly full of it in Fargo last year with that Runnel thing." Schade snorted. "Good Lord! How anyone . . . . *Sheesh!* Kids locked in cages in the basement!" Ross shuddered and yanked the car to the right, flooring the accelerator as they shot onto Interstate 22.

"That poor schmuck."

"What?"

Jack worked through a big mouthful of chips. "You know — the guy that wound up with the baby in his car. It'll take him a year to get untangled from that mess. Everyone thought he stole the kid."

"How'd they figure it?" Ross was in his element now, driving sixty-four in a sixty-five zone. Behind him a rusted van and its sweating driver slowed abruptly. Five other cars quickly fell into line.

Laughing to himself, Ross gradually accelerated to seventy.

"Somebody got a tip about the mother. Turns out she kidnapped the baby from the father, then tried to make it look like he was stealing the kid. But turns out HE was the one who should've had custody. And he would have, too . . . in another five days."

"Well that's a switch."

"Yeah. Fathers always get the rap." Jack sighed. "Now — just because of bad timing, he's going to have to wait awhile to get his own baby."

Ross brightened. "Hey, did you hear who got a promotion?"

Jack sighed. There would be no more quizzing about missing babies. If Ross knew anything, he wasn't talking. Jack would have to do more digging on his own.

Another long night. Another sleepless day. Tony's days and nights were one continuous blur, and it didn't look like things were going to change anytime soon. He was ready to snap if anyone looked at him the wrong way.

His mind was playing tricks too. Lately he thought he'd seen first one car and then another, hanging about three blocks behind him as he drove home from night shift. On two of those pre-dawn mornings, they'd followed his exact route, fading just short of Dakota Apartments.

It was almost noon, and by this time Tony should have been deep in slumber. But not this morning. Tony glanced longingly at his bed, every sinew in his body aching for sleep. Jake was up. Again.

First, he'd been hungry. It had taken Tony five minutes to warm the bottle slowly in hot water as Beth had taught him, then fifteen minutes for Jake to finish his lunch.

Then the baby had howled for thirty straight minutes, his body rigid, arms quivering. Beth had demonstrated how to massage the little guy's tummy and work out the gas bubbles, and at last it had worked. Tony and Jake both got three hours of sleep.

Then Jake was poopy and wet and howling again. Tony nearly lost his breakfast on that one. More rocking, more walking the floor, more massaging. Then . . . well, Tony wasn't sure, but it looked like Jake just wanted company.

"Oh Jake! Just . . . go . . . to . . . SLEEP!" Tony's voice rose a couple of notches and he gritted his teeth in frustration. Jake's lower lip turned down in a quivering pout and he began to breathe rapidly.

"Jake, Jake . . . . Sorry, old man." *Uh oh. I'm losin' it.* Tony looked around frantically for inspiration. He popped in an old Felix Esparsa tape of his mother's and took Jake on a gliding tour of the apartment. For fifteen minutes Tony held the baby, gently dancing to De Colores and La Cucaracha.

Jake fixed his eyes on Tony and tugged at the edge of his blanket with tiny fingers.

Good grief! Now I know I've lost it! He fixed Jake with a grim smile. *Here I am dancing with a baby and singing about colors and cockroaches. Definitely not chick-magnet stuff!*

In Apartment 212, Nina Manelli sat quietly in her frayed blue wing-back chair, shoulders hunched. Her Meals on Wheels driver was due and she was getting impatient. Nina hungered for the first sound of the key in the latch, then the sight of Marv's tall frame coming through her apartment door every day at eleven-fifty-five.

She'd given him a key on the sly, so she wouldn't have to pull herself out of that blasted chair. If she could just get her noon meal without the slow, painful walk to the door, if she could just one time a day talk face to face with a real live someone who seemed to care about her, even if it was only for five minutes — then she could get through the rest of the day until darkness came.

At night her daughter Elise would sometimes call from Los Angeles and they would talk for ten minutes. She would tell Elise that she was just fine, and then Elise would tell her all about the children.

And after that her daughter-in-law Rochelle might call from Cincinatti and Nina would once again pretend that all was well.

That was the way her days went, one after another, from Sunday through Saturday. But sometimes . . . sometimes when she did not expect it, her son Jimmy would drop by, full of bright chatter and a small gift.

At last, the friendly click of the lock, and Marv's booming voice rang out. "Mrs. Manelli! You're looking as beautiful as ever today. Is that a new dress? No? You could have fooled me! Very *very* attractive."

He kept up the patter while he opened the folding tray. He flicked a napkin off the dining room table, and opened the drawers where Nina kept her silverware, because Nina had drawn the line at plastic forks and spoons. Eight grandchildren smiled down from photos above the hutch.

Marv lifted the plastic dome off the brown institutional tray and tucked a napkin under Nina's chin. He patted her shoulder and looked her in the eye. "Need anything, Mrs. Manelli?" He paused, waiting.

How Nina yearned to ask him to do some little job for her. She winced and straightened. "There is just one little thing. It's such a lovely day. Would you please open my patio door? I'm having trouble with the latch."

Marv trotted energetically over to the sliding door and opened it wide. "Yes, it's a perfect day. I think we will have an early Fall."

Nina nodded her head. "Thank you, Marv. I'll be all right now. You have other lunches to take." She forced a smile and watched him open the door. Marv paused, and turned to wave. And it was just then that Nina heard something she had never heard in Dakota Apartment Unit Two. She heard a baby crying.

8

A pair of binoculars hid the cunning eyes of Jimmy Manelli as he sat parked across the road from Dakota Apartments. A gnarled oak canopied his gray panel truck so that only the windshield and front fender protruded.

Jimmy focused on the east side of Building Two, where sixteen balconies hung like shopping baskets over a sloping lawn.

Sweat coated his hands and he worked several long moments to bring the southeast corner of the building more sharply into focus.

The last ten days had been agony for Jimmy Manelli. He'd told Furman Adams that the baby was dead — that he'd put the the infant into a steel box and hidden the whole package in a deep cove.

But surely Furman Adams wasn't buying that story. No. Furman must know. He knew everything in Cedar Bend. Mayor Adams had connections to everything and everybody in this city. Oh yes, he knew. So why was Jimmy still wearing his head?

He wiped the sweat from his forehead with one sleeve, then with three stubby fingers adjusted the lenses until he could see with exquisite sharpness the deck outside Apartment 102.

Jimmy spotted two plastic lawn chairs, one picnic table and a gas barbeque grill behind the deck railing. Draped over one chair was a blue bib emblazoned with "I love my Daddy." A pair of sunglasses sat on the picnic table next to a half-empty glass of tea.

Hanging from the gas grill were one fly swatter, a burger flipper and a meat fork. Barely visible on the back of the grill's propane cylinder was a putty-like gray lump with two insulated wires protruding from it.

Behind the deck, glass sliding doors were tightly closed against the afternoon sun. But the drapes were partly open, and Jimmy's binoculars panned slowly back and forth, tracking Tony as he walked in and out of the living room, carrying a bundle in his arms.

Jimmy smiled and stroked his chin.

The little "item" was in residence today.

Tony had never been so tired. Fourteen days of working at the hospital, then endlessly carrying Jake and changing diapers and warming bottles and trying not to yell was worse torment than getting stomped with cleats in a whole season of baseball — worse torment than trying not to fail English. Every muscle ached, and the temptation to let the baby scream while he succumbed to blissful sleep was overwhelming.

Jake had slept a good portion of the night while Jack Kowalski snored in his comfortable bed. But Jack had left for work soon after Tony came home dazed from a grueling eight-hour shift. Jake was now refreshed from a long nap and ready for action.

Tony — woozy and exhausted — had paced the floor all morning. At noon he prayed with every ounce of his being for just one hour of uninterrupted shuteye. His throat was scratchy and his ears ached.

And, no two ways about it, he was getting paranoid. He locked his Jeep and zipped the windows wherever he went — something he'd never done before. Once in the mall he'd bumped shoulders with some steely-eyed guy who got behind him in the checkout, then followed him into the next store.

Tony had taken to calling his father from work. Did he lock the doors. Was Jake okay. "Just wanna see how things are going."

Jack had not been pleased. "I'm sleeping, Son. Jake is sleeping. We're all sleeping. We'd like to keep on sleeping."

Tony sighed. "Okay, enough's enough!" He flexed for action and scooped up Jake, a fresh bottle and clean clothes. He'd try the tub. Maybe it would relax the kid. Tony set the cold bottle of milk inside a half-filled bucket of hot water and set it floating as the water rose. He'd thought of that little trick himself, much to Beth's surprise.

"Jake my man! Time for swimming lessons!" A laundry basket lined with an old flannel sheet went into the bathtub next, where it filled with three inches of bath water — another Tony original (*Sheesh — this is scary! I'm getting good at this!*). He lay Jake on the flannel and grabbed a wash cloth, then brought his voice down to a low monotone while he slathered on the soap.

"You are getting ver-y, ver-y slee-py . . . ve-ry, VER-Y slee-py." Jake responded with two flips of his arms and a bubbly fart. Tony laughed — good medicine for an aching body — while Jake looked up with his wise little frown.

WHUMP! The explosion shook the building to its foundation, shattering double-paned deck doors and shooting lethal glass spears across the Kowalskis' kitchen. In the bathroom, soap baskets and shower rod snapped, cascading plastic curtain and shampoo bottles over the tub.

Tony leaned his body forward in one protective motion as chunks of plaster fell from the ceiling, and glass from the mirror shattered over his legs and feet. He could feel Jake's little fists tensing against his shoulders.

He groped for a towel and engulfed Jake in its folds. As dust sifted from shattered drywall, Tony yanked at the bathroom door. He pulled again, panic rising in his gut. Jammed! Beneath the door, acrid smoke curled along the tiles, blending like chocolate syrup with blood from his feet.

Tony's ears were nearly paralyzed from the blast — he could barely hear yelling from the apartment hallway. All the sounds came to him as if he were underwater. Jake yowled, his face a muddy purple, but Tony could barely hear him. He jammed a towel against the base of the door, then searched frantically for an escape route.

The window! But he'd never squeeze through — not unless he took out the casing. And there wasn't time. Was there?

Tony ripped open a vanity drawer. Gasping, he shook the contents and fumbled through them, thankful they never cleaned out the junk — shriveled toothpaste tubes, pennies, gum wrappers, spent razors, nails — and a tiny Phillips screwdriver!

He grabbed the laundry basket and stripped out the wet sheet, then bundled Jake in a towel and thrust him back in the basket. He hefted it onto the toilet lid, away from most of the smoke.

"Augh-gh-gh!!" Tony howled as more glass shards dug into his bare feet. He stood frozen for two horrible seconds, afraid to move. Then he ripped the shower curtain off the rod and spread it across the glass-strewn floor. Nearly sobbing now, he sat on the plastic and with trembling slippery hands tore glass from multiple wounds.

Trailing blood, he balanced on the edge of the tub, then jerked open the window and jammed the Phillips into the first screw of the casing. Four stubborn screws, each one tight and unyielding against his shaking hands — and Jake bellowing with huge shuddery sobs so loud that Tony finally heard him.

Through clenched teeth he forced the comforting words: "Jake, Jake, it's okay, it's okay. . . . Wait. . . . *Here.*" Quickly he stuck the luke-warm bottle into Jake's mouth and propped it inside the bulky towel. Hands clutched in tiny fists, Jake hiccuped and sobbed and took a few pulls on the milk, then spluttered and continued yowling.

Tony balanced on the tub rim, barely holding his footing against the slippery blood. This time, screws began turning one by one. Tony yanked out the little casing and threw it outside. He could barely hear a faint crackling of fire in the outer rooms and hallway. More smoke seeped under the door.

Clothes! I need clothes! He banged open the hamper and stuffed Jake's clean shirt and diaper into a dirty pillow case, then crammed greasy jeans and sweat-stained T-shirts on top. He forced himself to pause, rubbing Jake's head for two precious seconds. Between hiccuping sobs, the baby's frowning eyes were mutely accusing. Good. Give Jake a few tugs on the moo juice, then haul him out the window.

Police. Fire trucks. Their siren wails floated through a long tunnel. Any second now and the apartment complex would crawl with cops and firefighters. Would his father come? Tony didn't know, couldn't chance it. This was no accident. Whoever did this would be looking for a man and a baby. He had to get out of here.

Tony's body screamed for action but he forced himself to move slowly, tying the pillow slip onto his belt, then holding the bottle in one hand with the towel-swaddled Jake in the crook of his arm. *Wait. Can't get through the window this way.*

Nearly frantic, Tony set Jake with his bottle and towel into the pillow case, then lowered it through the tiny bathroom window. The little bundle dropped the last two feet with a faint thud onto soft grass.

Tony squeezed into the opening, stretched his arms outside the window and pulled hard. Now he was halfway through . . . and stuck. He shoved his arms against the opening and pushed himself back into the room, then ripped off his jean-shorts and tossed them out. This time he scraped and pulled against the window, biceps quivering, and fell beside Jake. He lay for a moment breathing hard, then grabbed shorts and pillow case and streaked for the woods.

Behind the first clump of trees he stopped to get his bearings. A group of pines to his left, then a bike path. Three hundred yards of trees between him and the bus stop at College Avenue.

But first he'd have to get dressed and figure out a way to keep Jake from crying. He opened the pillow case and propped the bottle into the bundled clothes again. Jake flipped an arm out of his towel. His little scowl frozen in place, he finally began drinking.

Tony could see little specks of movement through the thick trees as he struggled into his clothes. He could hear sirens, but they seemed miles away. He dashed through the trees hoping he'd hit College Avenue at just the right spot.

His breath was coming in big gulps now, and his thumping heart nearly strangled him. He could see blood coursing down his legs and ankles, but he was numb to the pain.

Jake, finally exhausted and with the first edge of hunger satisfied, relaxed to the rhythm of Tony's pounding feet.

Across the cul de sac, Jimmy Manelli sat low in his panel truck. A rising sense of horror followed his gaze to the top of Unit Two, where hungry flames danced from Tony's ground floor living room toward the second floor.

In Apartment 212, Nina Manelli gripped her chest, then slumped in her chair.

The police radio crackled. "Backup. Backup. 2326 Dakota. Gas explosion." Jack Kowalski screamed at Ross. "Gun it! Rock 'n roll!" Ross clapped cherries on the roof and rammed his beefy foot against the pedal.

The Crown Victoria shot out of River Road towards First Street, then screamed onto Hubbard Avenue, siren wailing. By the time Ross and Jack pulled into the cul de sac, the first floor of Dakota Apartment Unit Two was a roaring mass of flames. Four teams of firefighters grappled with heavy hoses near the outer wall and into the apartment's hallway, while two ambulances waited for carnage.

Jack slammed into the crowd, elbows pumping. Tripping on the bottom step, he crawled and choked and stumbled into the burning building. Ross was close behind.

"YOU! Get back! Get OUTA here!" Ray Burgess, water streaming down his fire hat, contorted face angry and soot-flecked, stood like a granite pillar, arms wide.

Jack slammed him against the door frame and grappled his way into the burning hallway. "My son! My son's in there! Where's my son! Where's the baby! Tony! TONY!"

Ross grabbed Jack and spun him around. "Get outa here, Jack. If he's here they'll find him. If Tony's alive he'll want you alive too. Jack! JACK! Listen to me!"

Back in the car, Ross Schade wiped the soot from his eyes. He was about to ask his new partner, "What baby?" then changed his mind.

Jimmy Manelli slowly turned his panel truck into the side street and headed for College Avenue. He could no longer bear to watch those bright flames working their way towards the patio door of Apartment 212.

Tony raced through the woods, hugging the pillow slip tightly to his chest. Jake had stopped crying and was hiccuping in tiny jerks as Tony sprinted along the path. The bus was coming. He could see it flickering in and out of the tree line. *Oh God, oh God, oh God, just a few more yards. God, let me make it in time. Just a few more yards. Please. Just a few more yards.*

Met Transit driver Wally Meunch slowed, then picked up speed as he saw the empty sidewalk near the metal bus sign. With one gigantic effort, Tony sprinted and yelled with all his strength. Wally slowed again, the wheeze of brakes and tippy-tap of diesel-fed pistons marking time as this newest passenger staggered up the steps.

Tony faced the driver, gulping air. "How much to Jefferson Street?"

Wally's eyes narrowed as he studied his new customer. He took in the grimy hands, the bloody feet, the plaster-flecked hair and the dirty bundle. There was a dress code for Riverside Transit — "shoes and shirt required"— but to tell the truth he was a little scared of this wild-eyed guy, and today he'd make an exception.

"Dollar twenty-five." Tony put a trembling hand into his pocket and drew out five quarters, grateful he'd planned an afternoon excursion to the laundry room.

Tony stumbled to the back of the bus, trailing blood. Sleepy-eyed passengers stared, then lost interest. A homeless guy with a dirty bag. They'd seen it all before.

But Wally saw more than the ragged passenger retreating in his rear-view. He'd seen something moving inside that bag, and when he got off work he'd have a juicy story to tell his buddies at Jimmy's Pool Emporium.

9

Jake moved his lips in little smacks, remembering the warm milk. Softly he hiccuped. Was he in the car with Mama? No, this was different. There was vibrating and tingling and his ears felt full and strange. Every now and then a faint gasping, sucking sound came from somewhere under his dark little bed, and for a moment he remembered another time when he was cold and terrified, and rough hands grabbed his bare shoulders. He frowned and whimpered. No, this was not Mama's car.

But where was he? That man who laughed and whirled him around. Maybe he would pick him up now, and move him through a wide space of cool air into that bright light where the little chirrupy sounds tickled his ears and made him smile inside.

Jake could feel a stinging in his right arm, and he did not like the smell of this dark bed. It was musty and stale. And he was moving — swinging a little back and forth, then bumping with soft thuds against a hard place, against that distant vibrating sound. But his tummy was full and he was clean and warm and dry, and he could not keep his eyes open against the heavy force of that comfort.

Jake sighed and sank into a long tunnel of sleep.

Tony slumped on the back bench of the bus, mouth open, still breathing hard. He tried to keep the bag open a little, checking furtively inside for his little stowaway, and from time to time burrowing deep inside to make sure the baby was warm and that his face was uncovered. Occasionally a passenger turned to stare.

Tony felt the pain deepening in his legs and feet now, and the burning, searing fire of that pain shocked and sickened him. His whole body trembled. His stomach churned and his head spun.

Tony was gripped with a sudden panic to get to Beth's house before he blacked out. Illinois Street. Hickory Avenue. Another four blocks to Jefferson. He fought back a wave of nausea.

Wally kept adjusting the rear-view so he could fix Tony's face in his mind. There was nothing moving inside that cloth bag now. Maybe he'd imagined it. But he didn't imagine the blood stains on the side of it. Jefferson Street. Good. This was one passenger he'd be glad to get rid of.

Tony staggered from the bus stop, backtracking down the sidewalk towards Beth's house as the bus wheezed out of sight. His head spun and his ears buzzed. Everything he saw — everything he heard — seemed faint and far away. Somehow he got to Beth's front porch and rang the doorbell. Then he waited and rang again. No answer.

Next door, Leon Knox, recuperating from a broken arm, nudged the lace curtain aside. Two young girls living next door by themselves. And that wild man staggering on the front step. Maybe he should call the police.

Frantic, Tony pressed the buzzer and pounded on the door. "Beth. . . . Beth. . . . *Beth*," he croaked. "Open! Beth, please . . . please . . . open!" Then as a sickening tide of vertigo washed over him, Tony crumpled against the iron railing. He could feel his fingers loosening on the pillow slip, but could do nothing to stop the precious bag from sliding into the bushes below.

In the back room, Beth tossed on her bed in restless sleep. Her peaceful dreams had taken an abrupt turn. Someone wanted her help. She could hear a man calling, but where was he? The voice came from the ceiling, from the walls, from the kitchen. Suddenly, Beth sat bolt upright.

Tony! Tony was calling. She careened down the hallway, shaking off the heaviness of sleep. She lowered her eye to the peephole and scanned the front step. No one. She started back down the hall and then she heard it. A baby's cry. She knew it well. It was Jake's.

She yanked open the door, then shoved the screen against something hard. Tony groaned. "Beth . . . Beth. . . . Jake. . . . He's. . . . Beth. . . . *Get him.*"

"JAKE!!?? WHERE!? What did you do with Jake! Tony, what's the matter! Where is he!" Then she saw the white pillow slip in the bushes. "He's in THERE!!?? Wha. . . ?" She leaned over Tony, nearly squashing him against the railing, and pulled up the pillow slip. Jake was wide awake now, his whimpers tinged with anger. Beth raced inside with him, laid him on the sofa, then sprinted back to get Tony.

"Hang onto me." Beth struggled through the door with Tony draped onto her shoulders.

Leon carefully smoothed the lace curtain back into place and picked up the phone.

Beth dumped Tony onto the bed. "Don't move. I'm gonna take care of Jake."

Don't move. Yeah, that's it. Don't . . . move. He wouldn't have to. The room was spinning nicely on its own. *Yeah, don't move. . . . Don't move. . . .*

In the living room Beth got to work. "Gotta clean off that blood, Kid. Look at you!" Wrapping Jake in a towel she held him in her left arm while she filled a rubber dishpan.

It would have been easier, she later decided, if Jake had yowled his head off. But when she lowered him into the water he held his body rigid, his arms stiffly out to the side. His face was contorted, eyes wide with fear. Slowly she poured handfuls of warm water over his body, murmuring and humming, forcing her own body and voice to relax.

"You've been through a lot, Little One. . . . Sh-h-h. This is your Auntie Beth. You'll be all right. . . . You'll be all right. . . . Sh-h-h-h."

Slowly Jake's arms yielded to her touch. He frowned and began to study the gentle face above him. The rest of the world receded as he felt the warming laps of water and her practiced hands. Beth lifted him out and quickly wrapped him in a giant bath towel. She was tucking in the last folds as the doorbell rang. Beth muttered to herself. *Whoever's out there, I'm not home!*

"Okay, Jake. Let's put some medicine on that cut."

Now there was a pounding on the door, insistent and forceful. "Open up. Police."

Uh-Oh. Think fast, Beth. Holding Jake tightly against her side, she strolled down the hall and painted a smile on her face. She opened the door wide. "Yes?"

"Everything okay here, Ma'am?" The cop peered past her down the hall.

"Well of course. Why wouldn't it be? I'm just ready to put this little one down for a nap."

"Your neighbor says you might have trouble. You alone?"

"Oh!" Beth forced a chuckle. "I'll bet he saw my brother! Kane's a great practical joker. He likes to rattle my cage. Something different every week. Today he smeared ketchup on his legs and tried to make me think he was dying!" She pointed down the hall. "He's in the bedroom asleep. You can see for yourself if you want!"

"No Ma'am, that's okay. Just checking. Sorry to bother you."

Beth controlled the urge to slam the door, letting it click softly into place. She'd reacted with pure adrenaline in the last ten minutes. Now she felt the crush of real fear and her heart pounded.

What had happened to Tony and Jake? He'd said something about an explosion. What would happen now that her nosy neighbor had seen them come into her house?

And her roommate. She'd have to make up another story when Julie came home in four hours.

Tony and Jake would have to get out of here.

She pulled back the towel and stared at Jake's arm. What had made that gash? *Oh, dear God, I need help!* Should she call Jack Kowalski? Nope. No calls to the police station. Not even to Jack.

Leon saw the policewoman smile and stroll back to her car. No, no. That wasn't right. There was something going on next door. For one thing, he knew there wasn't any baby or boyfriend living at Beth and Julie's house.

Leon was seething with questions. He'd quiz his wife when she got home from work.

10

Someone was moving his leg. Someone was crushing him, lighting a torch under his feet. His throat was a flame of fire.

Tony licked his parched lips and moaned. "Jake. . . . Jake. . . ."

Now the torch was gone but strong hands held him down, sticking needles into his heels.

"Water . . . water. Get me water!"

"Tony, I've got you. Chill out, man. I hafta get this out." Skillfully Beth pulled four glass shards from Tony's legs and feet. Mouth open, breathing hard, she held Tony's knee in a vise grip while she worked on the tiny spears with her tweezers.

Suddenly she gave a triumphal thumbs-up. "There! I got 'em all!" Beth exhaled heavily and pulled a little metal tube out of her pocket. Tony could feel the cool antibiotic cream threading along his feet and legs, then the gauze strips and the bandages. Thirstily he gulped water from the sport bottle she'd shoved into his hand.

"Drink as much as you want, Kid. You've lost some blood. I'll bet you're dehydrated." Beth sat back and surveyed her handiwork. "I gave you Tylenol a couple hours ago. Remember that? You were burning up. Now just go back to sleep, okay, Tony? You're scaring me to death."

"Jake. . . . Wha. . . . Where's Jake?" Tony raised his head in panic, then let it drop heavily onto the pillow. The room wasn't spinning quite as fast, but he was still dizzy. Sweat ran in rivulets down his chest.

"He's asleep in that drawer." Beth poked a thumb over her shoulder. "At least it's better than a box!" She shoved Tony's shoulders back onto the pillow. "Now *sleep!!*"

———————————

Tony wakened with a jolt. Something wasn't right. A strong moonbeam poured through the cracks of the venetian blind, but a flitting shadow fractured the light in rhythmic motion — back and forth, then stopped. Then back and forth on the outside of the house. Tony watched it for a moment, struggling to make his brain work. His head felt like a bowling ball, and his neck was stiff.

Cautiously he lowered one foot to the floor and twisted his body into a sitting position. A searing pain shot up his leg. He gasped and clutched the mattress. Carefully he lowered the other foot and tried to stand. His heel was full of fiery darts where Beth had dug with that little surgical weapon of hers. He sat breathing heavily, trying to get up enough nerve to stand.

Suddenly he knew what was different. He could hear! There was a tiny tapping against the window, and a whiffly breathing coming from the middle of the floor. Had Beth put Jake on the carpet? Tony winced as he maneuvered towards the open dresser. He froze. His right foot was pressing into something soft and warm. He inched back and looked down. The moonbeam cast a soft fluttery glow, and Tony stared, his eyes slowly focusing in the dim light.

That thing on the floor was Beth.

She mumbled and sat up. "What're you doing?"

Tony let out a long slow breath and eased himself back onto the bed. "Where's your roommate?"

"Out with a date. I stayed in here with the door shut, but I heard her come home to change clothes a few hours ago. She thinks I'm at work. She never saw my car — it's in the garage." Beth yawned and scratched her armpit. "Thank God Jake was asleep!"

"What time is it? When's she coming home?" Something wrenched in the pit of Tony's stomach. He had to get out of here.

"It's eleven fifty-two." Beth's brow furrowed. "She has to work tomorrow. I don't know why she's out so late."

"What about you? You're supposed to be at the hospital."

"I called in sick." Beth was sitting on the bed now. "But you're the one who's sick. You shouldn't be up." She reached out her hand. "Let me. . . ."

Tony wrenched his arm away. "I'm not staying. I'm taking Jake and getting outa here." He scowled, staring at Beth, working up his courage. "I need your car."

Beth's whisper was urgent, panicky. "But . . . but Tony . . . you're hurt — and you're real sick, man! You can't just pick up and leave!"

Tony's shoulders crumpled and he fell heavily onto the pillow.

"Hey, what's the matter! Are you okay?"

"Yeah. I think so. Gimme a minute"

"Doesn't sound like it." Beth laid a hand on his arm. "If you're so fixed on going somewhere, I've got an idea."

Tony lay still, scowling.

"My Aunt Frances. She's in Liberty. Kinda weird in a nice way. She and Ralph are always taking in strays."

"Who?" Tony's brain was about five steps behind.

"Strays. Stray kids, battered women. Stuff like that. I'll let her know you're coming and she'll have you in a warm bed so fast you won't know what hit you. Good with babies, too."

Tony snorted. "Yeah. . . . Guess that's as good as anywhere. Help me throw some stuff together."

"Wait, Tony. Just wait. Please try to sleep some more. You can go in the morning."

Tony grunted. "I'm leavin' now."

"But you could black out on the road! You're really sick!" Beth looked around the room wildly, stalling for time. "And we don't have a car seat for Jake."

"Look. A car seat is the least of my worries if those goons find us. Remember what Randy said? There are at least three of them. Maybe more. If they could blow up my apartment they can get to us anywhere."

Tony rubbed his eyes, then sat up. "I'll put Jake on the floor and hope I don't hit anything. Help me get some things together."

He paused, taking mental inventory. "Uh oh. What about milk?"

"You're in luck, my man. I was over at Milanda's this morning. You've got enough for twenty-four hours. She gave me a sack of clothes, too. Some for when he's bigger. And yesterday I snagged some diapers from MegaBarn."

Tony started to get up, then sat down abruptly. The room was beginning to spin again. Somehow he'd have to stay conscious long enough to make the forty-minute drive to Liberty.

Suddenly the front door slammed. They heard a faint clunk as Julie tossed her car keys onto the table, then the tingle of closet hangers.

Tony froze.

Beth put a finger to her lips and slowly shook her head. Then they heard the bathroom door close. "She's as predictable as sunrise. Next she'll take a shower. We've got twenty minutes."

Beth turned on the table lamp, groped around in the drawer of her nightstand, then pressed some keys into Tony's hand. "Get in the car. And pray that Jake stays asleep. I'll get some stuff together. If she sees me I can make up a story about coming home on break. But I sure don't know how I'd explain *you!*"

Tony hobbled painfully towards the hallway.

"Tony! Wait! Here!" Beth disappeared behind the sliding closet door, then emerged with a wad of T-shirts, some grimy sneakers, two pairs of sweatpants and a jacket. She shoved them into Tony's arms. "Don't worry. They'll fit."

From the driveway Tony stared at the bedroom window. Back and forth, back and forth against the panes, a dark branch tapped and scraped. Gratefully he pulled on the flannel-lined jacket. The nights were unseasonably cold for the last week of August, and Tony shivered with fever.

He turned towards the garage and flipped up the door, then eased himself into the front seat of Beth's rusty Honda. With exquisite care he slipped Beth's sneakers over his wounded feet, gasping as they squeezed the bandaged flesh. Leaving his shoes untied, he slumped against the seat, head drooping.

After a moment he spotted Beth's cell phone on the car seat. The urge to call his father was overwhelming, and he nearly sobbed with longing. Maybe he should call. Maybe not. . . . Was it safe? His brain started fuzzing up again. *Dad . . . Dad. . . . Don't give up on us.*

Suddenly the passenger door creaked open. Beth was loaded to the chin and breathing hard. "Quick. Grab Jake. Lay him on the floor in this blanket. He's still asleep." She threw a sack of clothes into the back and plopped a plastic cooler next to Tony.

"Here." She thrust a tiny crumpled note into Tony's hand. "Frances. Address and phone number. And here. Keep this bottle in your coat pocket. It'll warm up quicker." She started to back out of the car. "Want me to talk to your father?"

"I don't know . . . don't know. . . . Just . . . just wait. I'll get Frances to call." He moaned, shifting his foot.

"Tony, I. . . ." She reached into her pocket. "Here." Beth laid a wad of twenties on the dashboard.

"Beth, you can't. . . ."

"Shut up, you!" Tears streaked down her face. "Just get outa here. Go. *Go!*" She closed the car door and ran for the house.

11

From the time she was five years old, Helene Pardiac Morrow had been aware of her power. As a little girl in Tupelo, Mississippi, she had carefully studied each person who entered her life. She had paid particular attention to the raised eyebrow, the smile or the frown, the way this person or that one delighted in her presence.

And she soon discovered that they were soft clay in her hands.

She had taken special delight in her little brother Billy. He followed her everywhere, begging for attention, joining in her made-up games. She learned to use him as her backup, to make sure that he always got the blame. Billy was always there. Billy could take the punishment. Billy never tattled.

At age ten, Helene could sometimes be found in her room, primping languidly and practicing sweet expressions before the mirror.

At age thirteen she had begun using her graceful figure and luminous eyes to gain power over boys and to revel in the side benefits of destroying confidence in the other girls at school.

At twenty-three she had walked away from her short marriage as easily as throwing a candy wrapper in the trash, clutching her firstborn to herself. She was finished forever with that fleeting feeling called love. She had begun to use, instead, her feminine magnetism to put cash in her wallet and bring men to their knees.

But at age thirty-two her ability to deceive men had taken a sour turn. She had met Dr. Benjamin Quaid. At first it had been easy to manipulate this puppy-dog of a man, who had begun each morning with only one motive — to please Helene Morrow.

She had toyed with him, often ignoring him for days, knowing he would knock at her door the instant she called. Best of all, little Marianna had adored him, and Helene had found temporary relief from bringing up the little brat by herself.

One year into this poisonous alliance, Helene was the one who had knocked on Benjamin Quaid's door. She was four months pregnant, in need of a quick solution.

Benjamin had yielded.

He had given her what she wanted. Then, frightened of his plunge into a world he had vowed never to enter — he had left Helene in the private hell of her bedroom to wrestle through the aftermath of a saline injection while he sneaked back to the hospital to deliver babies.

She had endured the endless night alone.

The pain for Helene on that August night had been both frightening and deep. She had groaned and writhed for seven hours before bringing forth a tiny pickled-red boy, salt-scalded and dead. She had gritted her teeth, dropped the remains in the garbage, and vowed revenge on the man who had left her to suffer alone.

She had waited six long years before the opportunity had unfolded at her feet. Six long years in which Helene had become increasingly aware that her beautiful body was flawed. Helene's timing for revenge was at its peak now, because her daughter Marianna was pregnant and the last thing in the world that Helene wanted was a less-than-white child calling her Grandma.

Carefully she had forged her plan. She had reminded Mayor Furman Adams that his precious college son had seduced a sixteen-year-old girl — statutory rape any way you look at it. She had reminded Dr. Benjamin Quaid, as she had every one of those six years, that the hospital board might wish to be enlightened about the private medical procedure performed by their Chief of Obstetrics.

The plan had been flawless. By the sixth year of her suffering she had inflicted the maximum torment on Benjamin, while ensuring for herself a generous profit from drugs channeled through Morrow Imports by the good mayor of Cedar Bend.

Subjecting Marianna to pain had been a minor hurdle. But the girl was young and she would adjust in time. Sacrificing the incidental child had been the easiest part of the plan, and Helene had scarcely given it a thought.

Now Helene's careful scheme was unraveling because that easiest part of the plan was not only alive — it was an ever-moving target — and none of the dolts in charge of its demise could tie their own shoes or spell their own names.

Helene would need reinforcements.

She would call her little brother Billy.

12

Tony yelped as he pressed the gas pedal. His foot was swollen and throbbing, and each movement brought fresh pain. Squeezing the steering wheel, he grimaced and eased down on the pedal, backing out of the shadowed driveway in little fits and starts.

He narrowly missed a parked SUV and a tower of stacked garbage cans.

The old Honda whined in protest as Tony shifted into Drive. The gas tank was only a quarter full but it should get him to Liberty. Sweating from every pore, he slowly turned down Jefferson, then onto Twelfth Avenue and headed for Main Street.

The dashboard clock glowed a sickly green. Twelve-twenty. Five hours until dawn.

In less than a mile he was weaving through the narrow strip of stores by the river. The old brick buildings were dim and empty except for two bars and their lingering hollow-eyed patrons. Street lights, tall and gaunt, sent spindly shadows across the pavement.

By the time Tony came abreast of the blinking light in front of Union Bank, the pain had settled into nearly tolerable numbness. He'd learned quickly to keep steady accelerator pressure and pace his approach to traffic lights. Anything to avoid braking and moving that blasted foot.

As Tony eased onto First Avenue, he caught a pair of headlights in his rearview. He pushed the little Honda to fifty, then sixty, praying the lights were not attached to a police car.

No ID. A wad of loose bills. And a stowaway kid. Just your ordinary, hard-working guy out for a midnight ride. Tony's sudden laugh was brittle and tight.

Another turn south onto Highway 56, then east on Interstate 22, and the single headlights behind him blended with traffic. Tony punched the cruise control at sixty-five.

After ten minutes his head nodded with fatigue as the landscape stretched into a monotonous ribbon of asphalt.

Jake had slept deeply for three hours, and now he was aware of the humming motor. Cushioned in a pile of sweatpants and shirts on the floor, his little arms twitched spasmodically as he dreamed of his favorite pastime — eating.

His lips smacked.

Then one eye opened.

He squeaked a little to get the attention of the guy above him.

"Huh?" Tony flipped his eyelids wide, panicked that he'd nearly dozed off. He mumbled a pained reply. "Awake, are you?" He reached for the bottle. Uh oh. Still cold.

Man, we're in trouble now! Tony knew Jake's timetable. A couple of squeaks, then a wail, and in five minutes he'd be in full cry. The kid was probably sopping wet too, but Tony didn't dare stop. Not now.

Quickly he stuffed the bottle under his armpit to warm it up. That did it! Now he was as wide awake as the baby.

Tony checked the rearview again. Two gargantuan semi trucks eased into view. Now and then he could see one headlight poke out from behind the pair of eighteen-wheelers, then recede.

The icy bottle under his armpit was warming about as fast as February snow, and Jake was past his little patient squeaking. He was howling and shuddering in great angry sobs.

"Okay . . . okay. Please, Jake. Here, my man, let's try it cold, okay?" Tony pried off the plastic cover with his teeth, then propped the bottle against a bulging fold of sweatpants. Jake pulled hungrily on the nipple, swallowed and spluttered, then howled his anger.

"Sorry, man. Okay, okay. You'll be glad to see Frances, little guy. I'm sure she won't pull this stuff on you." He eased off the highway, crunched onto the shoulder and set the car in Park. He tried to move quickly but he was breathing hard and struggling just to lift his arms. He fumbled for a clean diaper and went to work.

"You've gotta wait, Jake. . . . *please*." Tony gritted his teeth. Pain and fatigue tugged at his patience, and his head began to whirl again.

He reached behind him and scrounged in the sack of clothes until he found a pacifier. "Best I can do. Hey, man, just chill out, Okay?"

Jake accepted the little plastic holder with its rubber nipple after a couple of tries, then hiccuped and frowned, staring hard. Tony eased back onto the highway and with a sudden smile at his new-found wisdom, popped the milk bottle against the windshield and cranked up the defroster as hot as it would go.

His smile was short-lived. Even the few moments he'd spent attending to Jake had relieved the pressure on his wound. Tony nearly screamed aloud as he once again pushed on the gas pedal. Trembling, he checked his rearview. Another vehicle had pulled off the shoulder onto the asphalt about a quarter mile back, its lights off.

Tony kept the Honda down to forty-five for about ten seconds. The car behind him accelerated onto the highway, its lights still off. Tony sped up, and the vehicle in his rearview gradually pulled closer until he could see a gray outline of the driver's face through the windshield.

Tony was focused so tightly on the mirror that he missed the

Liberty turnoff. "No! No! No!" He banged the steering wheel and sped up in panic. Sixty-five, seventy, seventy-five. The car behind kept pace. Where was the next turnoff? Maybe Colchester in twenty-five miles — but where would he hide in that little city after midnight? The police station?

Ridgeback State Park, next right. Tony waited until the last possible moment, then yanked the little car to the right where it bumped and clawed its way across the steep gravel triangle onto the exit ramp, spraying rocks, engine whining. Behind him, he caught a glimpse of the mystery car as it flew past the exit — a silver Chevy Suburban.

Tony's right leg trembled so wildly he could barely hold the pedal to the floor, but somehow he managed to whip north onto County Road 47 and crank the little car up to eighty-five.

No cars in the rearview. He nudged the Honda to ninety.

Suddenly, a glint of moonlight bounced off something shiny about a half mile behind him. The Suburban, its headlights still off, was gaining fast.

"Two can play this game." Tony doused his lights and kept the protesting engine wide open. The two sparring vehicles sped down the slumbering county road like medieval ghosts in armor.

From his left Tony gradually became aware of a light flickering among the trees. Intense and focused, It was moving straight for him. Then, about a quarter mile ahead, two blinking red lights suddenly lit up the night. Railroad crossing barriers fell into place and the glaring light on his left was joined by a rumbling blast.

A coal-black engine bore down on him, grinding slowly but relentlessly towards the crossing. The Honda was pushed to its limit but Tony knew it could not beat that train to the crossing . . . *could it?*

"Oh God, oh God. Please. *Please. . .* !" Tony first began to brake, then clamped his teeth and rammed the gas pedal. With a sharp intake of breath he rammed through the barrier, thumping across the tracks as the deep-throated whistle blasted near his head. The

Honda slipped and scrabbled across rails and ties, then bounced crazily onto the pavement as the black engine brushed the edge of the rear bumper.

Tony trembled, his sweating hands clamped tightly to the steering wheel, injured foot jamming the gas pedal. No response. With slippery hands he cranked the ignition hard, the starter grinding in protest.

Three times.

Four.

Then it caught. This time he met his pain head on, yelling as he stomped the pedal. Jake wailed too, and the triumphal, guttural screams from inside the car were a rally cry of raw courage.

On and on they flew, north towards the park. He was grateful for the train that had nearly ground them into hamburger. Those mile-long grain haulers could take several minutes to maneuver a crossing. But just as he passed the tiny sleeping town of LaGrange, he spotted the silvery reflection of a vehicle again — this time less than a mile behind.

Ahead, a brown wooden sign with yellow lettering pointed to the right. "Ridgeback State Park 2 miles." Tony jerked the steering wheel savagely onto Avenue C and sped eastward. On his left a dumpy farmhouse sat gray and dark near the road. Tony made an instant decision: Pull into the driveway.

The weeds were waist high, blanketing the driveway, swishing and tapping against the Honda. Suddenly Tony knew where he was: Several times he'd seen this abandoned farmstead on his way to the park.

Behind the house was a huge drooping barn with gaping holes and sagging roof. Fallen doors lay drunkenly in the weeds. One of them leaned precariously against a peeling metal gas barrel.

Tony eased the Honda inside, crunching through empty chicken coops and dirty straw, squeezing past an old Ford tractor hunched in the corner. He peered at the road through a broken window. A loud screeching chilled his gut. The Suburban had just made the turn onto Avenue C. It passed the little farmhouse like liquid silver.

He's coming back. For sure he's coming back! Tony looked through the barn door and studied the empty house, his breath coming in short hot gasps. Maybe he could hide there with Jake for half an hour until that maniac gave up. His mind raced through the possibilities. Maybe the water hadn't been shut off — his thirst was a growing monster and his head pulsed in great thumps. Tony quickly scanned the road from the broken window, then stumbled for the house, moaning with every step. He would check things out before carrying Jake inside.

Mammoth weeds grew between sidewalk squares, crowding the sagging wooden steps. An L-shaped extension of the house shielded him from the road and barn.

Tony clutched the wobbly brass knob and gently pushed. The door creaked loudly in protest. In the old kitchen, a beam of moonlight illuminated the cracked linoleum, and a musty smell of old wood and mouse droppings hung in the dead air.

A galvanized spigot squeaked under his touch. Dry as dust. He clutched the sink rim and lowered his head, gritting his teeth in agitation.

He and Jake would not be safe here.

Better to risk the open fields. The barn would shield them in those first precious seconds.

To the north and east Tony thought he'd remembered a cornfield, then a vast open pasture and a grove of giant oak and walnut trees in a crazy patchwork of steep rock outcroppings. There were caves all over this area.

If he could just get Jake inside one of them.

Tony staggered back through the weeds to the car. He could hear Jake wailing. Frantically he stuffed food and clothing into the old pillow slip, then ripped a jagged air-hole with his teeth. "Jake, Jake, little guy. Listen."

Tony held the baby close to his face and rubbed one of the tiny shoulders with a grubby thumb. His voice was shaky and erratic. "You gotta . . . be quiet, okay? I know . . . I know you can . . . can do it. Just do it for me — Uncle Tony."

Jake stared hard, and in the dim moonlight Tony could see the wise little face puckering for a howl. Then, as if turned off by a switch, he seemed to change his mind. He accepted the lukewarm bottle and the musty pillow slip.

Jake sighed and sucked on the milk. This guy was hard to figure. But once again, he was dry, he'd heard a beloved voice — and finally — someone had gotten the message that he wanted warm milk, not cold.

Tony's face twisted in anguish. How did he get right back where he'd started twelve hours before — running forever with a dirty pillow slip, a tiny baby and his feet cut to ribbons? His life was a sleepless cycle of running and suffering and screwing things up.

13

Billy Davis Pardiac slammed on the brakes. He glared at the sturdy iron barrier blocking the entrance to Ridgeback Park. Fuming, he took quick practiced note of the terrain. Behind the gates, black outlines of trees blurred together into dense forest.

A rim of low bushes, rock outcroppings and scrub trees spilled out of the park on either side of the entrance, and on the south side of the road they stopped abruptly to join rolling fields. To the north, scrub trees continued into a ravine where they united with towering oaks and maples. With the exception of the one cornfield he'd passed near the turnoff, the rest of the surrounding land was in pasture.

Billy focused on the iron gateposts. They were nearly flush with two giant burr oaks which shouldered the barrier. No room for a car between those. The kid didn't get this far. With one fluid motion he put the Suburban in reverse, spun the wheel and headed west on Avenue C.

Billy patted the gray duffel bag as he accelerated. He'd get his prey. He always did. He'd seen only one farmhouse on this back-woods road. That kid and the brat had to be there.

Billy set his jaw and deftly guided the steering wheel with one hand, scanning empty meadows on either side of the road. A wizened dead tree hugged the south fenceline, its skinny arms tracing jagged black forms on the ditch.

There. To the north. He could just make out a small house near the road, with its broken-down barn off center to the northeast. He cruised slowly west past the driveway a few yards and rolled silently to a stop. The farmhouse now lay directly between him and the barn.

He ran one hand expertly through his duffel. He pulled out a 9-millimeter Glock 17 pistol and pulled the action, loading a round in the chamber.

Quietly he nudged against the Suburban door and glided out and down, like a snake in the weeds. He hunkered low to the ground, listening and sniffing the air.

Billy had a good view of the house just north and to his right. He took in each detail — three gabled windows on the second floor — two on the first, with the front door squarely in the middle facing the road. One corner of the barn was visible behind the house.

———————————

Tony lifted his precious cargo out of the Honda just as he caught a gleam of silver through the barn window. The darkened Suburban was prowling west down the road, back towards the farmstead.

It slowed, nearly stopped. Tony sprinted out the east side of the barn, battling thistles and milkweed. Then he crouched low behind the short line of trees, gasping and storing up a few ounces of strength for the next few yards.

Again a few more yards, then another faltering stop to catch his breath. When he gained clear sight of the road, he trembled with relief. He could no longer see the shadowy Suburban.

———————————

Crickets chirped, occasionally raising their chorus to a crescendo. From time to time they stopped, leaving tiny black holes of silence. It was during one of those lapses that Billy heard the creaking hinges.

He glanced quickly at the front door of the house. It was heavily boarded. He hunched over and slipped towards the northwest side of the building, his stocky frame casting faint shadows onto the peeling white boards. He continued north and hugged the walls so he could approach the back door with minimal exposure to the barn.

Billy crouched low as he rounded the northwest corner of the house, his breath moist and heavy, his olive T-shirt ringed with sweat. All was quiet, including the crickets.

As he hunched towards the back door, Billy blended into the black-green landscape. An ancient sidewalk lay cracked and bulging, running parallel to a windowless wall. Waist-high weeds waved gently in the late-summer breeze, and Billy raised himself a little higher so he could see over them.

Suddenly he tensed. Not all of the tall grasses were swaying in unison. Leading straight up to the door was a trail of trampled weeds, some of them rising from the ground in slow, prayerful movements. Billy scanned the path. He could not see the trail of disturbed weeds all the way to the barn, but he figured it began there. He focused again on the back door, which swung in a slow arc, creaking loudly in the night breezes.

They're in there. I've got 'em, Sis. Billy snorted softly in anticipation and slowly turned his head towards the barn. There. On the west side. A rusty two-hundred-gallon gasoline barrel mounted on a metal stand.

Billy headed west from the back porch, then swung north towards the tank. He patted the barrel expertly. Still some fuel in there. Probably gas. He rummaged through the tall weeds until he nudged something light and hard. Two plastic jugs. He smiled.

Billy whipped out a long folded knife and slashed the hose, jerking back as the spurting gasoline sprayed his pant leg. As he filled the jugs he sneered in grim praise to the farmer who'd left a little fuel in this old tank.

The jugs were full now and he stopped once more to listen. A rustling in the cornfield. Was it wind? He waited and the rustling continued, growing fainter and fainter.

Just the wind.

Quickly he splashed a trail of gasoline from barn to house, then silently turned the second container on its side and slid it into the kitchen. He raced halfway back to the barn and snapped his butane lighter, then touched the flame to the gasoline-soaked grass.

Billy bolted for the Suburban and yanked open the door. He cranked the starter, jamming the pedal a half-second before the first *whoom* of orange flames rocked the farmhouse. Windows exploded as a giant fireball lit up the little dwelling for the last time. A couple of moments more and flames would explode the tank by the barn. He squealed onto the pavement and headed west.

At the first fiery *whump*, Tony instinctively crouched low to the ground and pulled the pillow slip against his chest. Within moments the house was a mass of flame. He raised his head just in time to see the Suburban accelerating towards Highway 47.

Tony pushed himself off the ground and stumbled and fell, then lurched into the cornfield. He flailed through the stalks for several seconds, gasping and sobbing. A second ball of fire rocked the earth with a louder thump, sending him sprawling.

He could hear the steady patter of burning fragments nearby. He staggered to his feet, dragging the pillow slip a few bumpy steps before he again lifted it to his chest. Tony's breath came in rasping wheezes, and his legs wobbled like wet spaghetti.

Somewhere below him in a long, long tunnel, Jake was crying.

He flailed and lurched and somehow kept moving, forever inside row upon row of corn. He'd eaten nothing for fifteen hours, and in his woozy half-dream the pain belonged to someone else. His body seemed to float over fiery-hot stumps. Cornstalks rattled as he rammed his way through, their sharp-edged leaves slicing his face like a thousand tiny whips.

Several times he fell, breaking the heavy late-summer stalks in his path. Tony ran blindly, unable to see behind or ahead. Just corn and more corn.

"Oh God, just the trees," he prayed. "Please . . . please get me . . . to the trees." Tony now focused on just one thing — that black outline of forest he'd seen from the road. It would be a couple of hundred yards ahead — if he were going in the right direction.

In the town of LaGrange, population four hundred and seventy-two, eight phones rang between 1:47 and 1:48 a.m. Dave Mackie yawned, stuck his arm out of the covers, and reached automatically for the receiver. "Yeah?"

"Fire at the old Keidel farm, 1055 Avenue C. Looks like a hot one. Whaddya got?

"Down to one truck. Get me some tankers from Berryville and Dunston."

"Yo."

Art Bellman gave his wife a quick kiss, threw on his pants and shirt, and raced out the door.

Matt Runkle, his head spinning from a late night in Colchester, stopped undressing for bed and put his shoes back on.

Larry Goudge called his mother. "Kids asleep. Mind comin' over?"

"On my way."

At 1:52 a.m., Truck Number Two headed out of the new steel building, roared up Main Street, then careened north onto County Road 47. Dave cranked up the sirens, and the lone truck, blaring against the night, had the road all to itself.

14

Now the air was cool and still, and the crickets had silenced their singing. A blanket of gray clouds covered the sky. On the crest of a vast dark meadow a broken figure clutched a dirty bag, then staggered and swayed.

No more . . . no more. . . . No . . . more . . . running. Tony dropped to his knees and loosened his grip on the bag. "I can't. . . . I can't. Oh Jake, I can't. I'm sorry. . . . I'm sorry."

He felt the bag slip from his hand as he lay against the pungent grasses, clawing feebly at the soft earth. Then he was still, but for long moments he dreamed of little Jake, helpless against that monster truck with its dirty diesel plume — coming ever closer. Then Mamita, running to push him away before she fell.

And Jake crying . . . crying . . . crying.

Slowly Tony became aware that someone or something was prancing in quick little steps about his head, its hot breath mixing with rivulets of cool night air. He could hear soft whimpers near his face. Then the dancing steps were stilled and a warm body pressed against him. Little driblets of saliva dropped into his ear.

Again the soft moaning, the heavy snuffly breathing.

Then a rumbling, deep-soft voice: "Veda. fetch the bag."

Huge stovepipe arms lifted Tony, and he felt the world waving and receding, trees looming, a tightening around his body.

Grunts, a heavy thudding and scrabbling as he chafed against heavy metal clasps. Ahead — or was it behind — Jake's cries mingled with whining and moaning, snorts and snuffles.

He drifted into a dark pit of blessed silence.

15

At ten o'clock on Friday, September First, Jack Kowalski walked straight past the refreshment bar into the office he shared with Investigator Schade. Mechanically he slipped off his jacket and shook out the rain. For some moments he stood at the window and stared at the steely landscape.

Ross was already at his desk, digging through a rubble of files. He got up, hesitated, then put his hand on Jack's shoulder. "You shouldn't be here, Buddy. You didn't have to come in today."

Jack stood rock still, his face muscles working rapidly. He swung around to face Ross, then swept his arm in a wide arc. "This may be all I have left. I've been back at the apartment a dozen times — talked with the fire chief — talked to the neighbors."

He smacked a fist into his open palm. "All they found was one sick woman. There were no bodies in the building or on the grounds."

He turned a glowering face towards his partner. "I just want to know. Where is Tony?"

His shoulders slumped. "If I stay in that blasted motel one more minute I'll go crazy."

"I wish you'd change your mind and stay with us." Ross folded his arms and looked away. "Lisa and I are praying for you."

There was a long, unsteady silence. "Yeah. . . . You go ahead. . . . Go ahead and pray."

Patrol Officer Lynn Fallows knocked twice, then opened the door. "Someone wants to see you, Jack." Ross settled back in his chair.

Lynn hesitated. "He wants to see you alone."

Ross arched one eyebrow, then pushed back his chair and headed for the hall. "I'll get a soda."

Jack stared at the husky kid in the doorway. That face under the baseball cap — he'd seen it before.

One hand lifted to remove the cap, and a shock of sandy hair fell to Beth's shoulders.

"Ah. . . . You're Tony's friend."

Beth breathed deeply, her fingers clenching. "Yeah. I'm Beth. Tony and I both work night shift at the hospital."

Jack tensed, waiting.

She glanced nervously at the door. "Mr. Kowalski, I'm scared. Real scared."

Jack walked over and clicked the knob. He motioned to a chair and forced himself to relax. "Sit down, Beth. Just take your time. What's going on?"

"Tony's been taking care of Jake. Well, you know all about that. Tony says you've been helping."

Beth shifted uneasily. "I see . . . I used to see . . . him every night at work. Last night — I mean yesterday — I think someone tried to kill them both."

She got up and walked to the window. Her voice cracked. "I'm sure they've figured it out by now, because . . . because. . . ." Beth covered her face with her hands.

Jack's face darkened. "What do you know about it?"

"Tony came to my house right after it happened. He. . . ."

"*Tony?* Tony was at your house?" Jack gripped the edge of the desk and tensed forward. "Did he have Jake? Where is he?"

"I . . . I don't know where he is, Mr. Kowalski. He's not there now. He was hurt pretty bad and Jake was cut too, and he figured someone tried to kill him and Jake. About midnight he left the house in my car. I told him he could hide out with my Aunt Frances in Liberty."

Relief flooded Jack's face.

Slowly Beth lifted her head. "But Mr. Kowalski, he . . . he never got to Liberty. My aunt hasn't seen him. "

Jack's mouth turned to paper.

"And . . . and . . . the reason I'm so scared . . . is . . . if someone figured out how Tony got to my house, they'd have to be . . . have to . . . ." Beth covered her face and choked down a sob. "They'll get all of us . . . *all* of us! I just . . . I just don't know what to do."

Jack sat a moment, staring out the window. Then he stood and faced Beth. "I know some guys in Dover and James Counties. Somebody had to have seen something."

He gripped Beth's arm and set his jaw. "I'll find them. If it's the last thing I do, I'll find them both."

"There's something else. I hate to bother you with this." Beth held out a set of keys. "Tony said I could use his Jeep. I gave him my Honda."

Jack leaned against the window frame, then slowly shook his head. "They know his car. I don't want you to be a target too."

"But I don't. . . . There's nothing else I can drive and I'm on duty tonight. I took a bus here this morning."

Beth wiped her eyes. "I'm sorry. It's been a pretty long twenty-four hours."

Jack relaxed his shoulders. "Of course — look, any way you figure it, we owe you a car. I'll take you to Westside. They'll give me a square deal. And when Tony brings back your Honda. . . ." Jack warmed to his own hopeful prediction. "Why don't you go out first. I'll meet you in the parking lot in five minutes."

Beth slipped on her cap and jacket and walked quickly through the maze of outer office desks towards the back door, head down. Lynn Fallows cradled her coffee mug and wondered just where she'd seen that kid before.

Jack waited a couple of minutes, then ambled to the refreshment bar and forced himself to sip slowly on a tall mug of coffee, no sugar. Ross eyed him warily.

Jack sighed. "You're right, Ross. I shouldn't have come in. I think I'll check in with the fire marshal, see if they've got any leads on that arson, then take a long weekend. See you after Labor Day."

Ross leaned one arm on the bar and watched Jack stroll towards the basement stairs.

Marianna sat in the school nurse's office clutching her belly. The tail of her shapeless flannel shirt was bunched in her lap.

Janet Borschell hovered nearby, checking Marianna's pulse, her mind a jumble of questions. Did Marianna really have the flu last week, as her mother's excuse note had said? And why had she been sick so many days last spring?

Now this girl had missed the first four days of the fall semester, and here she was complaining of abdominal cramps. Something was very wrong.

"Marianna, why don't you lie down here and I'll call your mother. You've missed the first week of school with that nasty virus. You're terribly pale."

"*No!* No. Don't call my mother. She . . . she can't come. She . . . left town this morning."

"But I have to call someone. What about a neighbor? Anyone?"

Marianna forced a weak smile. "I'll be okay. Really. I just need to lie down for awhile."

Janet hesitated. "Let's do this. If you're not better by noon, I'll take you home myself."

"Mrs. Borschell. . . ."

"Yes?"

"I'm sorry to be so much trouble."

Janet flashed a sympathetic smile and gently guided Marianna toward the bed. "You are *never* any trouble. You're one of my favorite people! Now. Down you go. This blanket will feel good on a rainy day."

Janet left the office and Marianna pulled the gray wool blanket up to her chin, turning her face to the wall. Slowly she brought her thumb to her mouth and curled her legs tightly towards her chest. She murmured a little tune while one slim finger twirled loosely in her long, flaxen hair.

16

*G*et up. Get up. Where is he. . . . Find Jake. Find. . . . If only he could move, he would do something. Anything. But his eyes simply would not open.

The fire. . . . Was Jake near the fire? He could feel it near his face and smell the smoke and hear the crackling. What was that sound? Little metal clankings and soft scraping sounds. Was it behind him? And that whine again, mixed with snuffling. But there was no murmur or cry from a baby anywhere, only the quiet little clinkings and snufflings and cracklings.

Tony could dimly remember the hours before — it seemed so long ago. There had been large rough hands and sharp earthy smells like the center of a forest. Someone had laid wet cloths on his feet and slipped something vaguely sweet under his tongue.

Then a new sound wove itself into the tapestry of his consciousness. It was a steady creak, creak, punctuated by little grunts and scrapes and mutterings.

Then Tony heard the sound he'd been waiting for and his eyes flickered. Somewhere close — or was it far away — he could hear Jake's whimpery hunger noises. But it was so hard to move! He willed himself to turn, strained to follow the direction of that sound.

Slowly and with great effort Tony made his head turn and he opened his eyes. He stared for a few moments, struggling to focus.

Near his bed, glowing branches crackled in a cavernous fireplace. Flames licked giant, strangely-shaped logs, and a gray-pink light shone feebly through a smoky window. Above the stones and blackened mortar a rough-hewn mantel jutted into the room, with a tiny electric lamp glowing at one end. Massive beams rose to a high point in the ceiling, then dipped sharply down the other side.

But where was Jake? With great effort Tony moved his head to the other side. His neck ached and his head was so very heavy. Slowly a vision swam into focus. He saw a huge shadowy form dipping slowly back and forth in time to the creaking. He could still hear Jake, but now the whimpers had been replaced with eager slurping sounds and little grunts.

"JAKE!!" he croaked in a hoarse whisper. "Jake!" Suddenly the creaking stopped.

"So. He wakes."

"Jake. . . . Please. . . . Where's . . . Jake. . . ?" Tony's whisper was hoarse and faint.

"I believe this is your little friend."

Tony could just make out the figure of the enormous man who occupied a broad-planked rocking chair in the corner. Tenderly the child was held up for Tony to see. Jake was nearly swallowed up in a heavy dark green towel, his puff of dark hair rising like a periscope.

Tony let his head sink back into the pillow. He swallowed and put one hand outside his blanket.

"Where . . . is this?"

The man turned his head towards Tony. "You are in my house. And we are at your service." The rocking resumed. "Veda found you on the meadow. You were about done for."

At the sound of her name Veda whined and lifted her head. Tony could just begin to see her now in the dim light — a black whiskery giant of a dog lying at her master's feet.

"How . . . long. . . ?"

There was a pause in the creaking. "Twenty-nine hours and five minutes. You have been asleep most of that time."

Tony struggled to rise. He gasped, gripped in a sudden panic. "Where did . . . where did you find . . . food for Jake. . . ? There wasn't. . . ."

"Oh, Sheilah was happy to share."

"Wha. . . ?"

"My goat. Jake has taken a great liking to her."

Tony melted back into the pillow and closed his eyes. His arms were like limp rags and he could barely move. But gradually an immense peace flooded over him.

He could trust this giant in the rocking chair. He would stop fighting, stop running. He would sleep. As he relaxed into a deep heaviness he could barely hear the man who rumbled softly in a strange musical accent:

"Sometime, my friend, you will tell me your name and why you are running."

———————

Deputy Marlin Malek leaned against the Dover County Sheriff's car and pulled up his collar. Behind the sagging yellow police ribbon lay a blackened wreck of smoldering timbers, twisted metal and scattered debris. A chilling drizzle spit and fizzed against charcoal cinders in what was left of Pete Keidel's barn.

A burned-out Ford tractor, its hood warped, leaned heavily on bare rims. A few feet away was the whitened shell of a compact car. No license. Marlin walked slowly towards the vehicle and inspected it on all sides. They'd find the license somewhere in these ashes. Nothing unusual, he figured — those plastic clips holding the plates were always the first to melt.

A white car slowed behind him and crunched onto the gravel drive. It sat awhile, its driver taking stock. Marlin walked over and leaned against the open window. "Morning, Gary. Looks pretty pat here. Except for the car."

Regional Fire Marshal Gary Cushek unfolded his long legs and stretched. "Hope that rain doesn't get heavy. It's been threatening storm since I left Rapid City an hour ago."

"Think it's meth?"

"Maybe. Where's the fire chief?"

"Working at the cabinet factory in Colchester. He wants you to call."

Gary put his hands on his hips and walked a few steps towards the barn. "How do you see it, Marlin?"

"The only wild card is the car. Gabby found the VIN and she's checking it now. Thought I'd stay and get you up to speed."

Gary moved purposefully into the ruins, pulling on a pair of rubber gloves. "Talk to the farm owner?"

"Yeah. He'll be here as soon as he can make it back from a meeting in Colchester. He doesn't have any idea why someone would want to torch his place."

Marlin folded his arms tight and scanned the wreckage of burnt timbers that were once house and barn. Meth lab. That's what everyone said. Budding young chemists from Riverside or Colchester or Liberty, blundering their way into a small fortune with drugs, looking for any abandoned house they could find. And when they were finished they'd burn it and move on. Only this time they'd made one mistake too many. That's what everyone said.

But Marlin wasn't so sure. Not after that call this morning from his friend in Cedar Bend. And not after he'd finally talked with Phyllis Keidel. She'd called Pete at the Dover County Watershed meeting this morning after her sister Rosie stormed into the driveway of their new homesite "spraying gravel all over the rose bushes." Pete would be home real quick, she said, and get over to the farm. No, she said, they didn't keep a car in the barn, just an old tractor.

So if that car belonged to the meth guys, where were its owners? There weren't any bodies. Someone had deliberately set this fire. You could still smell gasoline in the burnt timbers.

Marlin folded his arms and stood staring at the ruined farm site for a long time. He buttoned his jacket tightly around his neck. Why would the drug guys burn their own car — or even a stolen car?

He stood in the misting rain and looked hard at the corn crop which on this first day of September had already lost its summer freshness. Corn leaves rattled in the steady soft rain.

The field was a "half section" — three hundred and twenty acres, running from the north at Pete Keidel's new house on Avenue D, south to within thirty yards of the old farmstead. It continued east about three hundred yards, where it was bordered by Henry Sebastian's cattle ranch. Marlin sauntered over to the crop.

Absently he rubbed some of the charcoal between thumb and forefinger.

A narrow band of stalks was singed from flying debris, but thankfully there'd been enough green in the plants to keep the cornfield from erupting in flames last night. A month later and the whole field could have gone up in smoke. Marlin crossed about thirty rows into the towering stalks, then started slowly making his way south towards Avenue C.

The rain drummed more steadily now, hitting the ground in muted thuds, splatting on the stalks with a determined pat-pat-pat. Maybe this soggy earth would yield footprints, but they'd be harder to find as the rain intensified.

Marlin continued walking south, his lowered head moving from right to left as he examined the ground and the evenly spaced stalks. He crossed to the west between two corn plants and started south again. He paused, looking hard at the muddy soil.

He stopped suddenly and squatted, then reached down and pried up a sodden sneaker. It had apparently snagged in a ring of brace roots. He stayed low to the ground, turning it over in his hands. Even the steady rain had not been able to wash away the blood that saturated its fabric interior. He noted the label stamped on the rubber sole: "Shipmate." And the size: 10.

Marlin slipped the shoe into a plastic bag, then stowed it inside his jacket. This was evidence, plain and simple, and he had no right to conceal it — even for a few hours. But this shoe was also a lifeline. He would show it first to his friend.

The Deputy stood uncertainly for a moment, then suddenly changed direction. He stopped following the row as it was planted, from north to south. An irregular swath of jagged stalks, bending from west to east, had caught his attention. He'd follow and see where it led.

———————

Jake moved his mouth in and out with little pouting motions. He frowned in concentration. Here was a strange face. This was not someone he knew. But there was a steady peace in the strong arms, and that delicious after-taste of sweet milk surely came from some-place good.

After awhile he decided he did not mind the dark, flashing eyes and the rough whiskers that circled a smiling mouth. Perhaps the lit-tle snuffly sounds and the whiny noises came from the man too. Soon Jake was mesmerized by the cracklings in the fireplace and his own heavy comfort. He would sleep and maybe get a good look at this new guy when he woke.

———————

Marlin was working so hard to follow the erratic trail of bent and broken stalks that he was surprised to break out suddenly into a mowed strip — and beyond it, fenced pasture. He stopped, breathing hard, and surveyed the meadow before him.

About twenty feet from the last row of Pete Keidel's corn, a barbed wire fence ran north and south, separating lush grasses from the strip of mowed, gray-green weeds near the cornfield. He could see where the pasture ended to the south at Avenue C, but about a quarter mile north the fence mounted a steep hill, then disappeared. Marlin figured that at least half the livestock ranch was out of his range of vision, ending near Avenue D.

Running east and west, several more barbed wire fences intersected at right angles, forming at least eight different paddocks that Marlin could see. A number of galvanized water troughs hugged some of the fencelines in a clover shape, two tanks in each pasture.

The meadow had to end in a dwelling somewhere. He knew Henry Sebastian owned four hundred acres here, but where was the house? Surely it couldn't be down in the ravine which separated the meadow from Ridgeback State Park.

He took another step and leaned on a fencepost. Then something under the boundary wire caught his attention. Marlin stooped and fingered the barbs, studying the ground.

Even in the rain, he could still see a rubbed spot on the grass, and above it, a tiny shred of white cloth snagged in the sharp prongs. Marlin pulled the soggy bit of fabric from the barb and folded it into a second bag. Then he started back west towards his car. He'd try a different tack. He'd find the Sebastian driveway from the road.

17

Investigator Ross Schade stood on the concrete steps of 824 Jefferson Street, clipboard in hand. "Do you own a 1993 Honda Civic two-door sedan?"

"Uh, yes. . . . I . . . I do."

Ross studied the girl in front of him. This was the second time someone had been sent to this house. Not only that; he'd seen her before. But where?

"Good news and bad news, ma'am. We found your car at an abandoned farmhouse north of LaGrange. I'm afraid it was destroyed in a fire."

"What!!"

"Where was your car last night, ma'am?"

Beth began sweating heavily, her face a chalky white.

"My brother borrowed it. He . . . he said he parked it at the mall last night and it wasn't there when he came out. I was just getting ready to report it stolen."

"Whose car is this?" Ross thumbed towards the driveway at a 1996 white Buick LeSabre with temporary tags.

"Uh, mine. I was going to give my brother the Honda. I bought this one yesterday."

"I'd like to talk to your brother." Ross folded his arms and frowned.

"He . . . he went camping with a friend. I'm not sure when he'll be back." Beth forced a smile and wiped her face on her sleeve.

"Here's my card, Ma'am. I'll need you to come down to the police station and fill out a report." Ross clicked his pen. "I'll need your brother's name and a phone number where he can be reached."

"Uh, Kane. His name's Kane. Kane Lansink. And you won't be able to talk to him until he gets home. He doesn't have a cell phone."

Ross pocketed his notebook and pen. "Please have your brother call me when he gets back."

Dave! Gary Cushek here. I'm at the site. You guys had quite a bonfire last night. How'd you make out?"

"Thousand-carton marshmallow roast. Good thing we had those tankers from Berryville and Dunstan. Took us a couple of hours to get your barn site all prettied up for you."

Gary chuckled. "Yep. Your latest black on gray decor. Thanks." He flipped open his note pad. "Just a coupla questions. Did you see any traffic on Avenue C or County 47 while you were out last night?"

Dave hesitated. He remembered what Matt Runkle had told him — two vehicles streaking north on County 47 about one o'clock. But Matt was out late for all the wrong reasons last night, while his wife was home asleep. "I'll ask the guys."

"Well, ask them if they saw a '93 Honda Civic."

"What'd you find at the farm?"

"Gasoline, both buildings. Fire was hottest in the kitchen — you can still smell gas on the burned floor boards, and along a trail leading from the house to the barn. And it's pretty obvious how the barn was set. Must have been thirty gallons of gas in that old barrel when it blew!"

Gary clicked his pen shut, stuck it in a shirt pocket. "I checked for meth, too."

"No anhydrous or other meth stuff?"

"Nothing so far." Gary glanced at his watch. "Malek just left. He's doing a helicopter run to look for the driver. Could be someone on foot in one of those cornfields or even in the park. The ranger's got his eyes peeled too."

"I'll keep a lookout."

"Let me know if you hear anything else."

"Gotcha." Dave hung up, then punched in Matt's phone on the Frito Lay truck.

His body was being dragged towards the end of the bed. Huge hands locked around his ankles. And once again his feet were dangling in warm water. Tony knew what was coming next — the half hour of soaking, the large skillful hands and the deep-forest smell. His eyes flipped open.

"It's looking much better. Next time we'll get the clay booties."

"Hmm. . . ?" Tony had given up making much sense out of the lingo in this house. Nearly everything was a puzzle. It was as if he'd been born again, and just like Jake, he had to depend on someone else to teach him the basics of living.

Not since he was a baby had he been this helpless. He couldn't even go to the bathroom without being carried, and it was embarrassing to lie here hour after hour, on the makeshift bed right out in the middle of the living room where everyone could keep tabs on him.

"I'll get up. I'll be okay." Tony struggled to his elbows, but the violent shaking of his upper arms made him exhale rapidly and fall back on the mattress.

"Is it so wrong to let someone help you?"

"No, I just. . . . It's just that the sooner I get up and around. . . ."

"The sooner you get up, the sooner this infection will knock you flat. You not only cut your feet to ribbons, you also have a pernicious virus. Please let me finish with your feet. As soon as you are well you can go wherever you like."

"What . . . what's in the pan?" Tony had to admit the warmth was soothing.

"Magnesium sulphate. Some call it epsom salts. I'm just making sure your feet are perfectly clean before I bring out the clay booties."

The big man at the foot of the bed folded his arms over massive bib overalls and frowned. "Some of those cuts were very nasty."

Tony frowned. Man, his brain was working overtime. This was the weirdest place he'd ever seen — goats, a prehistoric dog, and a fireplace big enough to roast an ox. But he could sense that Jake was at peace, or at least he was eating like a baby pig.

Tony relaxed. He'd just have to put himself into someone else's hands — feet first. He closed his eyes.

Suddenly they popped open again. He was being watched. Someone was crouching at the foot of the bed, and he could see a little face and dark eyes under a mop of curly hair.

"Grandpa, did Peter fuss this much about getting his feet washed?"

"Yes, Molly. But he did it sitting down."

"Oh."

Peter. . . . Who's Peter? Well, I'm not going to ask. . . . I don't have the strength to work that one through my aching head. Besides, he had other things to worry about. Jake, snuggled inside his little bed, was beginning to fuss.

"Molly, hold this young man's feet down to the water. Yes, like so." The big man calling himself Henry Sebastian busied himself at the cradle while Molly moved front and center, stretching herself tall to the job. She was very good at her little task, Tony thought, but it was disconcerting the way she stared at him without blinking.

"What's your name?" Molly offered a shy smile, waiting for his answer.

Should he say? He wondered. But what was the difference between yielding himself totally into their healing hands and revealing his identity? He was completely helpless here, trusting Henry and Molly with his most prized possession — Jake. Surely they deserved to know his name.

"Tony.... I'm ... Tony."

"Hi, Tony."

Her smile was infectious, and so was the giggle that followed.

"Hi, Molly."

Suddenly the room was filled with an explosive sound, like twenty balloons releasing air. Jake was expressing his call to nature. Molly's mouth dropped open and she wheeled around. She dropped the pan of water and whooped.

Henry rumbled his deep-soft chuckle. "All right, Molly my dear. Fetch the towel from the sink. Fill the bowl again. Remember, not too hot."

Jake let out a bellow, then accompanied it with a second explosion.

From somewhere in Tony's weak body laughter began. It started at his shoulders and rippled down to his stomach. His mouth was open, his eyes were streaming and, weak as he was, he could not stop the spasms of sheer hilarity.

Molly straightened. "Oh Grandpa, look! Poor Tony, poor Tony!" And off she flew again, into a glissando of melodic laughter, only this time she shot towards the floor, slipping on the water.

Henry balanced the baby with one hand and mopped with the other. "Molly, take some clothes from the dresser in the pantry, child, and make yourself presentable."

The polished boots, the dark glasses, the slow walk. He was big — no two ways about it, and coming closer every second. In his side mirror Billy could see the trooper's right hand. It was dangling free.

One more inch and it would rest on his holster.

Just stay cool.

"May I see your license, please?" Sergeant Mike Jorgenson lowered his giant frame a foot or so. Now he was bending way over, practically jutting his face into the window. He was breathing deeply, as if he'd been running.

Billy Davis Pardiac smiled and nodded, pulling out his billfold. He fumbled with the little plastic sleeve, then lifted out the laminated card.

Jorgenson's glasses reflected a convex image of the silver Suburban. He studied the Mississippi driver's license intently for about five seconds, then flipped his head up to peer at the face. Back to the license. Back to the face. Another five seconds.

"Mr. Pardiac, Did you know you were going seventy-three in a sixty-five mile zone?"

"No, Officer. I thought I was going a little *under* sixty-five."

"I clocked you at seventy-three. I'm just going to write you a warning this time."

He gave Billy one last appraising look before returning to the patrol car. "It'll take a few minutes. Please stay parked while I process the ticket."

Billy breathed one long, slow breath as he watched Jorgenson's retreat in the rear-view. He leaned back on the head rest and closed his eyes.

Fifteen hours to drive from Tupelo to Cedar Bend. Another ten hours waiting for that slime-ball Jimmy to locate his quarry.

Then the chase in the country — another couple of hours. A quick nap behind a grove of trees. Now here he was at dawn, ready to cross the big river on his journey home. He could use a shower, a burger and a cold drink. But the need to reach Mississippi was a deep-gut urgency. He dare not stop again.

Billy was resting so peacefully that he did not hear a second patrol car easing onto the gravel, or the double click of two doors opening and closing.

But gradually he heard the returning footsteps. Heavier this time, he thought. More crunch, the sound coming from both the right and from the left.

He jerked awake and saw the second trooper, weapon drawn, easing up on his right. Billy fumbled inside his duffel for the Glock and fired wildly at the second trooper — just as a bullet from Jorgenson's Smith and Wesson ripped through his left shoulder.

The National Guard helicopter hovered over Pete Keidel's barn, then dipped to the east. Marlin Malek and Guard pilot Roger Westburg scanned each row of corn from north to south, then continued to Henry Sebastian's meadow. Below them in one of two dozen small fenced paddocks, a herd of Scottish Highland cows lifted their shaggy horned heads and bunched nervously near the watering troughs.

"Pull higher. Don't spook the cows! There. On the east side of the pasture. See that smoke? That's Henry Sebastian's house. How he ever got that place stuffed back in the rocks I'll never know. It's no wonder I didn't see it from the ground this morning."

Below, a cluster of barns, house and gardens was laid out like jewels in a crown. The house was nestled within a cliff-like outcropping, and the largest of the barns was all but hidden beside a steep rocky hill. Roused from dreamy slumber, a giant black dog bristled and snarled at the iron bird in the sky. And just as Roger and Marlin banked to return home, they saw a head poking out a massive door, and the dog running towards the house.

"I think I've got something. Can you meet me at Lou's Diner on Fifth?"

"On my way!" Jack leaped from the rickety bed and fairly flew out the door. Motel owner Virgil Benson watched as the black GMC pickup hurtled out of the parking lot. There wasn't a whole lot going on at Happy Trails in Cedar Bend, and this was about as much excitement as he'd get on a Saturday morning.

18

L abor Day weekend at Fifth and Main began slowly. Meg Sanderson and Belle Henley stared lazily into the window of Mae's Finer Clothes, then walked across the street to Finney's Super Valu. Five members of Colchester's Saturday Morning Breakfast Club shared a joke outside Lou's Diner before their coffee and pancake marathon.

Will Johnson waved a half salute to Marlin Malek and asked him what he was doing out and about on a day when he didn't have to work.

"When it's time to work, then work hard — when you got a rest, take a load off your feet," he drawled, his ebony face creasing into a grin. "C'mon in and have some pancakes. Put some meat on those bones!"

"I'm holding out for Carrie's raspberry pie. Tell her I'll be out one of these days to collect."

Marlin watched Will join the other four retired farmers, jostling and teasing and getting a head start on their tall stories as they crowded through the diner door.

Marlin stepped closer to the street just as Jack's GMC pulled up to the curb. He opened the passenger door and slid into the front seat — and the two old high school buddies clasped hands with quick, fierce affection. Marlin was shocked at Jack's appearance.

The boyish good looks were marred by sharply etched creases around the eyes and mouth. There was a grayish tinge to his skin, and the man looked like he hadn't slept in weeks.

Marlin turned away, embarrassed by the pain and naked eagerness in Jack's eyes. He fumbled with a plastic bag, then hesitated, afraid of the answer. "I just wondered if . . . this could be Tony's."

Jack took the sneaker and cradled it in his hands, turning it several times. He looked at the blood stains and winced.

"I don't know, Marlin. It's the wrong size, and it's a Shipmate. Isn't that a woman's shoe?" He sat motionless, frowning. "Last time I looked, Tony was wearing Reeboks."

There was a short pause as Jack stared out the window, concentrating. "Tony could have been barefoot when he got to Beth's house."

He set the shoe down and leaned forward, arms draped over the steering wheel as he talked through the puzzle. "I saw Beth a couple of times. She's a big girl. I wouldn't be surprised if they wore the same size."

Marlin nodded to the right just after they'd passed the small town of LaGrange. "Turn here. Go about a quarter of a mile. Okay, there, on your left, but don't stop." Jack slowed his pickup as they neared the burned farmstead, past a yellow police ribbon sagging across the weedy driveway. A white sedan was curtained under the willow.

Marlin motioned to the left. "There. In that cornfield. That's where I found the shoe. I figure he could've run out the east door of the barn and started across the meadow. Maybe just ahead of the fireballs."

Jack sat rigid, gripping the wheel and leaning forward, straining for something that looked like a trail, a clue . . . anything. He started to pull over.

Marlin tapped the steering wheel. "No. Just keep going. Cushek's not finished with his investigation, and there's been a lot of traffic through here the last couple of days. Let's keep this between us for now. Tony doesn't need any more trouble. Besides, I want you to see Henry Sebastian's place."

Jack eased the GMC up to thirty-five while Marlin gave directions. "Okay . . . right . . . *here*. Stop a minute. See that barbed wire where the pasture starts? See that bottom strand? That's where I found this. . . . Where is it. . . . Yeah, here it is . . . this piece of fabric." Marlin opened the little bag. "Looks like sheeting, or maybe a shirt."

Jack turned the tiny scrap of cotton over and over. "Can't say. It could be anything. I don't know what Tony had with him, and since the apartment was totaled I don't know what's missing."

Marlin studied Jack's face a moment. "Okay. Let's do this. . . . Keep going now, real slow. It's almost impossible to see Henry Sebastian's driveway. Go . . . go . . . go . . . okay . . . right . . . *there*. See where the gravel dips down from the road? See that iron gate at the bottom — between the trees? That's Henry's place."

They sat in the idling pickup studying the entrance. There was no mail box, nothing to indicate human habitation.

Marlin spoke first. "You game to go in?"

Jack leaned back and surveyed the landscape. "What do you know about this Sebastian guy?"

"Rancher. A little off the wall with his methods. Well-liked. Quiet. Good conservationist. The state's tried for years to buy his property and hook it up with Ridgeback. Just a minute."

Marlin pulled out a small notepad from his shirt pocket. "Uh, let's see. . . . Here it is. He wasn't born in this country. The park ranger thought maybe Spain or Portugal. Wife died a couple of years ago."

Marlin flipped another page. "He has a daughter and a bunch of grandkids living across the pasture there." He motioned to the north.

"Let's do it." Jack pulled into the steep drive and nudged the nose of his GMC up to the padlocked gate. Both men got out, trying to decide what to do about the barrier.

Jack glanced up and down the fence. "I don't see any signs. Let's just climb over and walk in."

They couldn't see a house or barn, just trees and more trees, and as they continued on the gravel, little droplets of dew flicked down from yesterday's rain. Well into the tree-shrouded driveway, Jack felt the quietness, punctuated by trilling bird calls and the rustlings of tiny creatures near the earth. And the fragrance. Like the center of a forest. It engulfed him in gentle waves, drawing him in, tapping in him a tiny chord that felt very much like hope.

But Marlin was noticing something quite different. "What are those boxes up there?" He pointed skyward and then Jack saw them too — a dozen or more long black boxes, suspended by slender pipes from the branches of maples, oaks and hickories.

Veda heard them first. A low rumbling started in her throat. Then, as if energized from the vibration in her chest, all the hairs on her back bristled into a massive brush. From her rumpled bed by the fireplace she rose and walked stiff-gaited towards the front door, lips curled back.

Henry intercepted with a low command: "Stay, Veda." The dog trooped back to the hearth and sat alert, still growling. Molly gripped one of Henry's massive fingers and looked imploringly at his face.

"Sit with Tony, Sweetheart. Wait for me." Molly trotted back and perched on the foot of the bed, swinging her legs. Tony felt little prickles of fear peppering his arms and back. He wished Jake was safely in one of the bedrooms instead of sleeping in a cradle right out in the middle of the living room.

Henry opened the inner door first, then clicked it shut and stepped into the entryway. He was not used to sneaking around, wary of intruders. Always his home had been open to strangers, to injured animals, to children of all ages. But today he had made up his mind to mask the truth and shield the young refugees inside.

Tony had yet to reveal his story, but the signs were all there. Henry had seen them before: struggle and flight reaching their long arms into his house. He would not betray his guests.

He opened the outer door wide and planted himself on the top step, arms folded across bib overalls. His massive frame filled the doorway. Nothing could be seen in the house beyond Henry Sebastian, and the two men facing him began to shift uneasily. Marlin flipped out his badge.

"I'm Deputy Sheriff Marlin Malek from Dover County. And this is my friend Jack Kowalski. We have reason to believe that a young man carrying a baby escaped from that fire down the road two nights ago and may have traveled east through the cornfield."

Marlin hesitated, stammering slightly. "Jack, here, is the young man's father."

Jack's face tensed up immediately, and he began clenching his jaw. Then he blurted out, "Have you seen my son, Mr. Sebastian?"

Henry eyed the two strangers. Before him was a so-called deputy sheriff without his uniform and a tall muscular man with military bearing. Could he believe these men? This Jack Kowalski did not look a thing like Tony. And why was he so fidgety?

Someone had set that fire at Pete Keidel's place. Someone was after Tony. Maybe these two men were the ones.

"You won't find them at this place, Sheriff. But if I hear anything that you should know, I will tell you." He went inside and shut the door firmly. They heard the bolt slide into place.

Jack clenched his fists, ready to pound on the massive oak door. Marlin guided him off the steps and urged him down the path. "Just let it be, Jack. If Tony's here, we sure as heck won't get past this guy without a warrant. We'll just have to do it another way."

Jack was trembling all over, both from rage and from crushed hopes. His mouth in a tight line, he began striding ahead of Marlin. Directly in his path, a plump black starling let out a sharp whistle, then flapped noisily into a darkened glade.

Jack stopped. He stood for a long time, his back to the house, head bowed. Then he raised his face to the sky and cupped his hands. He took a deep gulp of air and forced his breath into the narrow slit between two thumbs. A low hollow woodwind tone began quietly, then rose sharply and shrilly to a high piercing whistle. Jack continued blowing and lifting his top four fingers up and down while the eerie notes rose and fell in primitive cadence.

All over the woods, a backdrop of silence draped the powerful two-tone melody as the birds paused to decipher this new intrusion.

Marlin paused, uncertain.

Inside the house, a jumble of new sounds ricocheted against the pine-paneled walls. Jake wailed, Veda exploded in wolfish savage barking, Molly jumped up and down on the bed — and Tony hobbled painfully to the window, crying hoarsely, "Dad! I'm here. I'm here, Dad, I'm here!"

Henry plunged towards the window and scooped up Tony like a sack of meal. He flung open the door, and with the boy in his arms, bellowed down the driveway.

19

Jack fumbled for his ringing cell phone and flipped back the cover. He turned his head to muffle the sound.

"Jack, here."

"How's your boy?"

Tony's father smiled gently. "Asleep. Just a minute, Marlin, let me go outside."

"Got some news."

"Good, I hope."

"They nabbed a guy just this side of the river. Could be our man."

Jack gripped the phone. "Where is he?"

"Right here in Colchester. He's in for the grilling of the century."

"Give me an hour. I'll be there."

How many times over the years had he sat by Tony's bedside, watching the boy sleep. Now here he was again, watching over this child who had grown into manhood in one short summer. Jack's eyes brimmed as he listened to the peaceful, even breathing, mixed with Jake's little snuffles and snorts from the other side of the room.

He closed his eyes for a moment, remembering.

He had found Angelina in a Brownsville police station, where she'd been rounded up with eighteen other Mexicans who'd given their life savings for passage to America.

Heavy with new life, she had sat alone in a corner, her head buried in her arms.

He remembered as if it were yesterday, the moment she first lifted her eyes and held his own. They were eyes filled with suffering — but something else, too: a calm assurance, an eternal steadiness.

He had loved her and married her, had taken her child as his own — and then he had lost her the morning Tony stumbled in the street.

Head bowed, Jack whispered what he had never said in sixteen years. "You did not mean to fall, Niño," he murmured. "It was not your fault."

Tony stirred, opened his eyes. "Dad. . .? Did you say something?"

"I said I . . . want you to come home."

"Dad. . . ." Tony raised up on one elbow. "There's something . . . here for me. I need to stay awhile. "I've never . . . I mean I don't know why. . . . I just . . . need to stay."

"Of course. You need time to heal. I'll talk to Henry about it."

Tony fell back on the pillow, exhausted.

Jack winked. "You're not going to like who's doing your job at Shannon."

"Who?"

"Danny."

Tony groaned and shut his eyes.

It was nearly suppertime. Billy Davis Pardiac, his arm in a sling, had not stopped talking since they'd shoved the recorder under his nose at eleven-fifteen.

Deputy Malek sat in the stuffy interrogation room, watching Billy in morbid fascination. He'd heard the term "spilling your guts," but this was more like verbal vomiting. The longer Billy Pardiac talked, the more he seemed to enjoy it.

Billy's court-appointed attorney Mace Cagney sat slumped in a chair, tie loosened, collar unbuttoned. Lethargically he nursed a foam cup of stale coffee and stared at the wall.

This was a plea-bargain and a half, Mace decided. Billy had practically leaped out of his chair at the chance to implicate his sister and the mayor of Cedar Bend. They'd never get out of the slammer after Billy got through with them. *No way.*

Billy was through talking now. He punctuated his final sentence with a violent slam to the table as he snarled his sister's name over and over with such venom that Mace put up both hands, palms outward, and lowered his head in silence.

"Time for clay boots!" With a clatter of utensils and a shuffling of paper packets, Henry padded across the room from the kitchen. Tony didn't know how such a huge giant of a man could make the oaken floor planks fairly bounce under his advance, yet make so little sound with his footfalls.

"Let me see your feet now. Molly, bring that tray from the corner."

Here it comes. Tony's imagination had run wild the last twenty-four hours. What were those "boots" Henry and Molly were always talking about? He'd painted a picture for himself of great clodhoppers attached to giant braces.

But here was Henry with a small glass bowl and wooden spoon, stirring water from a pitcher into a brick-red powder. Then he crushed some green leaves into the mixture and stirred again.

"Ah. Here we are." A pungent fragrance like new-mown lawns filled the room as Henry tenderly patted the paste onto Tony's feet.

"That should take care of the rest of the healing." Then he motioned to Molly, who flipped out a long snow-white bandage.

Henry dipped his hands into a second bowl of water, then dried them on a kitchen towel.

"Wrap it around again. That's it. Not too tight. Good girl."

Molly lifted her face and smiled shyly at Tony.

"Now the boots."

From somewhere in her vast apron, Molly produced two plastic shower caps. Henry sprinkled a little more water onto the bandages before slipping the caps over Tony's feet. Then he straightened and planted both hands on his knees, looking vastly pleased with himself.

"There! And just your size!" Both Molly and Henry looked at Tony as if they were waiting for something. In the corner, Veda yawned.

"What's the green stuff?" *Oh rats. Why couldn't I just say "thank you" and shut up.*

"That's plantain. Grow it myself. When I was a boy in the Azores there was an old doctor who worked at the American base. I was an orphan." Henry paused, remembering.

"Dr. Manuel grew all his own herbs and used them on the injured pilots." Henry stared out the window, then rubbed his chin and winked at Molly.

"He taught me how to help him, just like my Molly helps me. One of the pilots brought me to America when I was twelve years old, and he let me raise those herbs on my own."

Henry went to the kitchen and got some jars. "Some of them don't grow here, of course."

He handed a container of dried chamomile to Tony. "But I found new herbs that I *could* grow."

"Buddy was sick and Papa fixed him." Molly beamed at Tony, trusting her simple testimony would convince him once and for all.

After an awkward silence, Tony realized he was supposed to say something. He cleared his throat and squeaked, "Who's Buddy?"

"Buddy's my pony. He got his foot caught in the lead rope and got all tangled up and fell down! He was making awful noises." Molly was standing now, gesturing wildly, her dark eyes round.

"Where did you find boots to fit Buddy?"

There was an incredulous pause, then Molly squealed into melodious laughter. "Boots to fit Buddy, boots to fit Buddy," she spluttered, before cascading into another warbling of giggles.

Tony could feel his body crumpling helplessly into laughter again. How good it felt to just let himself go. In a moment Henry chimed in with his sonorous bass, and the cavernous room echoed with their concert of joy.

The ribbon of asphalt from Colchester to Cedar Bend was boring, long — and about as lonely as any road Jack had ever traveled.

"Get over it," he said aloud. "Just get over it!" But he couldn't. A jumble of mental images wreathed like smoke in his brain. Jack sifted through the haze of thoughts as he drove, picking out the most compelling ones.

Mile after mile he drove, and within a half hour he'd managed to compress his memories into a compendium of failures. It seemed as if Jack's life had been all about losing. Losing his job in Texas, losing his wife, thinking he'd lost Tony — then finding his son only to lose him once more.

And, he had to admit, he was probably losing little Jake.

He knew Tony was safer at Henry's. The fire bug who'd torched the barn was locked up and likely to stay that way. But where were those "high officials" Beth and Randy talked about? Yes, maybe Tony should stay at Henry's. Danny could handle Tony's job for awhile.

It would all work out.

Maybe.

Jack knew all the "right" answers here, but his soul longed for Tony and the baby. Well, he hoped Tony would find what he was looking for at Henry's. He hoped it would work out better for the son than for the father.

Jack knew all about looking for happiness. He'd tried it and found all the wrong things. He'd found boredom, he'd found a place to lose his money.

Then he'd found a soulmate and he'd found God — and lost them both.

Loser. . . . A new little voice needled into his thoughts. *No, No, No. A thousand times NO,* he told himself as he gripped the steering wheel. He would not go down that path again.

But he did.

Near his bed that morning, Dr. Benjamin Quaid did something he thought he had long ago forgotten how to do. He got down on his knees and bowed his head.

20

've died and gone to Heaven. Tony stretched, yawned, and licked his lips. He'd slept the afternoon away, and now it was dark. He felt loose and limp and rested. In several days he'd be well enough, Henry had said, to help with the cattle. Best of all, his feet had all but stopped hurting.

Life was beginning to make sense. The peace, the joy of waking to a purpose. This was where he belonged. He just knew it.

What time was it, he wondered. Perhaps midnight, maybe three in the morning. He didn't care. No sense getting up until dawn. He stretched again, staring out the window at the dark-rimmed clouds as they brushed against the moon.

Near the window of the small room they shared together, Jake snuffled his little night-time noises. In that moonlit corner the heavy home-made cradle was a fortress — a staunch protection from the dread of the last few weeks.

Tony leaned back into the pillow and felt his body yielding to another round of sleep.

His eyelids drooped, opened a little, drooped again. Was the door to his room moving? It was opening so slowly that at first he was not sure. Was that a huge dark shape melting into the room? Whatever it was had stopped. Tony blinked, trying to focus. The shape continued to the left, towards the cradle and its little circle of gray moonlight.

The shadowy hulk stopped, bent down, and extended a long arm. Then the head lowered, and Tony heard mumbling.

Tony was so near sleep that he drifted in and out of a dream-like trance. There *was* a shape in the corner, wasn't there?

And it was bending over the cradle.

Suddenly, the shape straightened, glided back across the room, eased through the threshold, and the door was closed as silently as it had opened. Now Tony was fully awake, his body a mass of tiny prickles. He moistened his lips, then slowly moved one leg towards the side of the bed. Softly he slid his body over the edge, then tentatively stood and looked towards the door. Still closed. He limped to the cradle and peered over the railing.

Jake lay on his back, swaddled in Molly's hand-me-down pajamas. He moved his lips in little pouts, savoring the memory of Sheilah's bedtime snack. The little puff of curly black hair nested on top of his head.

Tony stood for a long time listening and gripping the cradle. Jake wrinkled up his face and sighed. In the living room Veda stretched and clinked her collar against the hearth. Outside, crickets chirruped a steady cacophonic backdrop for the occasional soft hoo-hoo of an owl. Soon the concert was joined by steady snores from Henry's room.

Tony bent over Jake and lifted him out of the cradle, then placed him carefully near the middle of his bed. He would sleep very close to this child tonight.

"You will come outside with me today." It was softly spoken — a command. Henry sipped his tea (what was that in that cup — something weird again) while Tony shoveled into his mouth a curious array of pancakes, garden fruits, mystery meats and some kind of strange white vegetable.

Tony shifted a little in his chair and turned to Jake, cradled in his left arm. He wrapped the blanket more securely over the tiny toes. "Sure. Okay. Do I . . . uh . . . bring Jake too?"

"We wait until he's asleep. Then Molly will watch him after school. It is too dangerous to bring him near the cattle."

Tony continued eating, watching Henry. Was he the one who'd stolen into his room last night? Or was he even sure he'd seen someone? Had he been dreaming? One thing he did know. If someone other than Henry had come into his room, Veda would have dispatched him in two bites. Yup. It was either Henry or a dream.

"Henry. . . ."

A pause on the way to the sink. "Yes, Tony."

"Someone was in my room last night." Tony suddenly realized what that sounded like. "I mean . . . I . . . wasn't sure. I could have been dreaming. But . . . uh . . . I think someone was standing over Jake's cradle. I don't know. . . . Was it. . . . Did you. . . ?"

Henry turned his back to Tony and continued towards the sink. Methodically he rinsed each dish, stacking them for a later washing. "I am sorry that I disturbed you. I thought you were asleep. I was simply doing what I have done every night for every child who comes into my home."

"What was . . . what was that?"

"I was praying." Henry walked to the door, plunked a floppy hat over his black bush of hair, then smiled broadly before pulling on his boots.

For once Tony was thankful for the loud squeaks coming from inside Jake's blanket. He busied himself with taking a small bottle of diluted goat milk from the refrigerator and setting it in a pan of hot water.

Henry's simple pronouncement was meant to reassure him. Instead, Tony felt a vague violation, as if he'd been shoved under a spotlight and made to give account.

"We'll take it easy your first day." Henry slowed his steps but it was obvious he'd prefer to trot from barn to house to field at a steady pace — just as he'd been doing since before dawn. Tony's feet were cushioned on makeshift sponge inner soles inside a pair of old boots. Henry seemed to have them in all sizes.

They crunched side by side down the gravel walkway to the first of two barns. When he came abreast of the north building, Henry motioned towards a twenty-foot doorway. Inside, Tony could see an old Dodge truck, a Case tractor, two all-terrain vehicles, a neat bench with assorted tools and a healthy variety of smaller equipment.

"That's the engine works," Henry said cryptically.

Thirty feet to the south, the two men walked slightly uphill to double oak doors which were closed at the bottom, opening in Dutch fashion to let in air and light from the top. Tony could already smell a faint sweet hay fragrance. Inside the barn, a soft whinny punctuated the quiet.

"That would be Carrot. She's just had a foal."

Tony peered into the dim interior. It was cool and clean. Carrot stamped a greeting and tossed her head, then continued munching her breakfast. "I use this barn for sick cattle or foaling horses — and for milking Sheilah. Scottish Highland cattle don't like barns. They'd rather have their calves right out in the open. So I just put up a few windbreaks in the fields."

Behind a four-foot fresh pine wall, a glossy chestnut mare with jet-black mane chewed contentedly on a wisp of hay. Warily she monitored the approaching visitors. Half hidden behind her, a foal, the image of his mother, peered anxiously. Tony walked right up to the stall, but Henry put out a hand.

"Go easy. She's nervous with that new colt. Just extend your arm real slow — let her decide for herself."

He murmured encouragingly as Tony reached towards the stall.

"Keep talking in a low smooth voice. . . . Yes, that's it."

Carrot backed her foal toward the corner, staring with huge liquid eyes. Tony kept saying her name and mumbling things like, "Hey, Carrot . . . what's up?" (What in the world do you say to a horse!)

With a sudden toss of her head she seemed to make up her mind. She took a few steps towards the hand and blew out a snort of warm breath. Tony was not prepared for the electric joy of connecting with the whiskery, velvet kiss. Carrot continued her snuffling investigation, then opened her lips to explore his fingers.

"Careful. She likes the way your hand smells. Thinks you've got something in there. Wait a minute. Here."

Henry fumbled in a steel canister and ladled out a dark mash. "Give me your hand." He poured a measure of the crumbly, sticky grain. "Now, just open your palm real flat and let her take it."

Tony lifted his hand again, and Carrot let out a shrill whinny. Behind her the colt shadowed her flank, peeking out with his narrow, comic face. There was no velvet kiss this time. Carrot thrust her nose into Tony's open hand, flapped open her lips and cleaned off the mash with practiced speed — then stamped her foot for more.

"Holy cow! What *is* this stuff?"

Henry chuckled low in his throat. "I make it up every day. That's oats, cider vinegar and blackstrap molasses. Be very careful when you offer this to our big four-footed friends!"

Elise clung tightly to her sister-in-law Rochelle and her brother Michael Minelli. Two times in the last two weeks they had made the trip to Cedar Bend. Two times they had stood before open graves, released now to say the words they should have offered to the living.

Elise clutched her shoulder bag, the tips of her fingers lightly brushing the return ticket to Los Angeles. She was ready, finally, to say goodbye forever to the city of Cedar Bend.

They stood bound together — arms entwined — before two gravestones and two mounds of fresh earth swelling up from the ground. The three of them read silently the handful of words they had already learned by heart.

"Nina Minelli . . . beloved wife, mother, grandmother . . . November 14, 1921 . . . September 2, 2005.

"Jimmy Minelli . . . beloved son and brother . . . August 5, 1960 . . . September 12, 2005."

———————

Jake felt the warm milk going down his throat, filling his insides with comfort. He gulped and chugged and sighed and clenched and unclenched his hands. He was cradled in a smaller space this time, and it kept jiggling. But never mind. The milk kept coming and he was getting more wide awake and excited by the minute.

When he was nearly full he began to think less about the milk and more about the vibrations around him.

He wondered about that sound. It was coming from above. No, it was coming from the side. Now he knew what it was! He wiggled one leg in anticipation. It was something good — he remembered that much. He could feel warm air brushing his face, in exact time to the little musical sounds.

Jake pulled his mouth away from the bottle. He lay very still, frowning and concentrating on the round face above him. He'd seen it before — the sparkling brown eyes and the merry, moving mouth — the bobbing head and the rhythmic squeaks and warbles.

Yes! It all fit together in a pattern. He was ready for this game! He knew just how to play it.

Only today, he'd try something different. He looked intently at the wide mouth. Maybe he could do that too. Jake stuck out his lips in a little pout, then sucked them back until he looked like a turtle.

No, that wasn't it. He'd try again, focusing on that wide grin bobbing around above him. Suddenly he found the exact muscle and his mouth pulled a little to the right.

"You can do it! You can do it! You can *smile*!" Molly's whole body jiggled with excitement as she bent low to plant a raspberry kiss on Jake's honey-brown neck.

21

The evening was strangely still. It was nearly seven-thirty and the dusky lavenders of the closing day filtered through the woods. There was an occasional chirruping sound, but the birds seemed reluctant to sing.

From the front porch, Tony hobbled out to view the dying day and breathe in crisp layers of cool air as they descended to earth. Everywhere he looked, birds clung to branches, darting their little heads back and forth as if waiting for something.

Then it began. Seven sweet silver sounds, stair-stepping their way downward, then pausing to begin again. It was some kind of instrument. Tony walked slowly into the trees. Now the birds were waking to a familiar call, because they all joined in at once — starlings and finches and robins and meadow larks.

Tony kept walking. The sounds enveloped him like mist and drew him on.

There. At this tree. A single violin, then another. The sounds were coming from up in the branches somewhere, pulling him along like a wave. Then he looked up. A black box hung from a hackberry tree. And on his left another black box, and another in front of him. Two on the other side.

"It's extravagant, I know." Tony about jumped out of his sponge-layered boots. Henry again. You never knew where he'd show up.

"The pilot who brought me to America always played this kind of music. I never wanted to be without it. So I brought it into the woods with me."

"The birds. . . . They . . . seemed to be waiting for it."

"They have come to expect it. Most nights at dusk, at least in the summer." Henry and Tony stood side by side, carried along by the incredible sweetness.

"I never play the loud music. Just quiet simple pieces, like this Adagio by Albinoni. Each one carries a memory for me. Gloria and I. . . ." Henry paused, swallowed. "Gloria and I played our violins together. She was the maestro. I just walked in her shadow."

Tony's insides were beginning to jump. He could not understand, nor did he trust, the emotions kindled by that one simple melody. He searched for words to match his feelings, and finally fell back on his old standby: "It's . . . really cool."

Henry smiled. "Yes. Cool."

———————

Molly was gone. She'd skipped home across the pasture. Henry was out somewhere, probably in the barn. The only sounds in the mammoth living room were the snapping of logs in the fireplace, and Veda snoring softly against the hearth.

While Jake slept, Tony slumped in Henry's overstuffed chair, arguing with himself. Of course he should stay with Henry. Dad would understand. It was still safer here than in Cedar Bend, wasn't it? Or was it just that Tony was almost happy for the first time in his life and didn't want to deal with stuff from the past. Sheriff Malek had called Henry, told him the guy in the Suburban was locked up — at least for now. Maybe no one else was after Jake.

Was this the end of his long journey?

But in his heart he knew he was still running. In the very center of his being there was no homing beacon, no way to know where he really belonged. For several minutes Tony sat frowning, his thoughts going in circles.

Absently he fingered the soft blanket and wrapped Jake tighter, then turned his face towards the sleeping baby. The little guy was freshly bathed and smelled like a morning sunrise. His tiny mouth was opened slightly, the breaths coming evenly.

Every now and then Jake thrust out his lips in a little pucker, then smacked them in memory of the sweet milk that always came from some magical place, just when he wanted it.

Gradually Tony could hear Henry's soft footfalls padding across the kitchen from the back door.

"What are you going to do with Jake?" One thing about Henry — he always got right to the point.

"I . . . don't know."

"But you do know something. Tell me what you do know." Henry lowered himself into the rocking chair, resting his elbows on the broad wooden arms.

"I . . . I think Jake really belongs to me. I can't explain it. But the funny thing is — I think *he* chose *me*." Tony edged forward on his chair, then got up and began pacing.

He paused before plunging headlong. "I'll make a home for him somewhere. The two of us — we're a family."

He jiggled Jake a little before pulling him closer. Then he stopped and faced Henry. "Could we. . . . ?"

"Stay here?" Henry folded his arms across his bib overalls, fixing Tony with a firm look. "No, Tony. You and I are tangled up in a fabrication. You cannot pretend forever. You and Jake cannot just simply take up a life somewhere. There is no way to explain who you are as a family — and until we shed the pure light of truth on this baby, you will never be free."

"Yes . . . but . . . I'm sure there are lots of things I could do." He stopped pacing and bent his head in thought. "I could. . . maybe change my name." More pacing. "Or what if you just told everyone this baby was your grandson, and I. . . ."

Henry stopped rocking. He smiled.

"Oh. Of course. Jake isn't . . . the same . . . as you."

"No. We're different colors." He waved his hand in dismissal. "That's nothing in God's big family. But that is not the central issue, Tony. The real difficulty is that we cannot prove where this baby came from, where his mother or his father are, or even if they would want him if we could find them. In short, he has no identity."

"But look at him!" Tony peeled back the blanket, revealing the tiny clutched fingers, the soft arm etched faintly with a silver scar. Jake frowned, then moved his lips rapidly in and out in a sucking motion, dreaming of dinner. "You just have to *look* at this kid to know he exists!"

"No, no. I didn't mean that. Of course he exists. Just not on paper, where it counts."

Tony paused to take this in.

"We must do this right or it will backfire." Henry got up and went to the window, pondering.

Then he turned and faced Tony. "I know a good attorney."

Tony's eyes widened.

"Don't worry. I'd trust Grace with my life. She's walked us through many a hard time. You'll meet her Sunday. She's even — what would you say — just like Jake.

"And Tony. . . ." Henry fixed him with a frown. "You must talk to your father about this. Do not leave him out."

———————————

One hour until dawn. Tony had been up with Jake three times, feeding him, changing him, trying to talk him into closing his eyes for a few hours. But Jake wasn't buying any of it. He was fed, he was dry, and he just wasn't sleepy.

Tony tried pacing, he tried jiggling him up and down on his own bed. He even tried one of Henry's secret weapons — gently rubbing his thumb across the eyebrows and singing deep, slow notes. *Nada.*

"Okay, Jake. Since you're awake — you're gonna hear about my last baseball game. Yup. It's the bottom of the ninth, we're ahead five to four. Northridge has two men on base — with two outs. I'm pitching and Robbie Gleason's up to bat. I figure he wants one of my famous low fast balls, 'cause that's what gives him the home runs."

Jake grinned and pumped his legs.

"Yeah. You bet it's exciting! Anyway, I'm thinking it might be a good idea to lob a slow ball, but I've never done it in a game before."

Jake frowned.

"Yeah. You know — the coach told me not to."

Jake gurgled.

"That's what I thought too. Anyhow, I can't get up the nerve to pitch that way."

Tony extended a finger and Jake clutched it tight. "I'm sorry, Jake. You probably know the correct term for a slow ball. I should have said 'change-up.'"

At Jake's frown, Tony chuckled. "Sorry to confuse you.

"So Anyway, the first two I throw wild so I can figure out what to do."

Jake murmured an encouraging "ee-yaw."

"You got that right. I can feel the coach looking at me. That's when I think — hey, I can do this! And I just let fly with a change-up. And you know what, Jake? It just goes right over the plate and Robbie swings like a crazy dude and misses! Hey, Jake! Gimme a high five — okay?"

In his room down the hall, Henry groaned and slid a pillow over his head.

———————

Tony and Jake finally fell into exhausted sleep about five o'clock.

It was nearly eight-thirty when they awoke to a sun-drenched morning. Henry had long finished milking Sheilah and moving the Highlands to their new paddock, and now he was pulling all the living room chairs and sofas into a semi-circle.

Molly and her mother Dora were dragging a few clunky folding chairs through the front door when Tony emerged yawning from the bedroom, absent-mindedly holding Jake with one hand, scratching himself with the other.

"That's my mom," piped Molly.

"Hi. I'm Dora. Don't mind us. We're just getting ready for church. Oh. . . ." She grinned and held out her arms. "This must be Jake. May I?"

Tony handed her the baby. No matter what time he got up, no matter how well he thought he knew this place, he always felt as if he'd just fallen through a time warp. He was learning to expect the unexpected.

Henry herded Tony into the kitchen. "This will just be our small group this morning. Our church is big but we meet in smaller cells once a month. This time it's my turn."

Henry groaned as a big sofa scraped the woodwork, then turned back to Tony. "I thought it was time this group met you."

Tony froze.

"Don't worry. Grace says it's perfect timing. You can't fight a battle like this by yourself."

He swept his arm around the room. "I trust everyone that's coming this morning. They're like family. In fact," he chuckled, "A third of them *are* my family."

A tall lanky man made his entrance just then with two dark-haired boys in tow. Henry nodded their way. "There's Hal — Molly's father. And that's James and Paul." The two boys crowded around Dora, laughing and chattering like parrots. One of them carried what looked like a wooden flute.

"Hey, Jake-O. Listen up." James coaxed a couple of notes out of the instrument and Jake's eyes widened. He breathed rapidly, his cheeks fluttering.

Hal laughed. "Hey James. Give the kid some room. C'mon over

here and help with these chairs."

Henry nudged Tony aside. "You might want to wear something besides those boxer shorts. This room's going to fill up in another twenty minutes. Molly can feed Jake."

At the sound of her name, Molly flitted over to the refrigerator and filled a bottle with goat milk and water. Tony backed up a couple of paces, then sprinted for the bedroom.

Good grief!

22

Carver leaned against the rough birch, eyes closed, lightly tracing his fingers on Marianna's arm.

The sun-soft breezes of early Autumn mingled with the pungent fragrance of damp earth. Behind them, a brick and native stone rest-stop hid the highway from view, but in the distance they could hear a faint hum of traffic and the occasional thunk of a car door closing.

"So much has been taken from us, Marianna."

Above them a birch tree rattled its dry-yellow leaves, dropping them one by one on the couple below. Suddenly Carver leaned forward, then glanced sharply at the young girl beside him.

"I don't think there was anything wrong with him. That doctor lied to you."

His mouth worked erratically and without meaning to he gripped her arm with almost savage fierceness. "Why did you trust him, Marianna! Why did you let your mother tell you what to do! He was *ours*!"

Marianna buried her head in her hands, the pale hair spilling across her knees. Her body shook with noiseless sobs. "Don't. . . . *Don't*."

Carver scrubbed one hand roughly across his face. "I'm sorry. Baby, oh Baby . . . I'm sorry. . . . I didn't mean. . . ." He put an arm around her shoulder and pressed his face against her hair.

Marianna rocked slowly back and forth, one hand gripping her belly as she murmured a tuneless song.

Carver held her in silence for a long time. Then he spoke. Slowly at first, choosing his words carefully. "Please just listen, Marianna. I know this could work." He flicked a tiny beetle from his creased trousers, then rubbed her shoulders lightly. "Didn't you say your father's name was Beauregard?" He waited to see what effect this would have. Marianna nodded her head a little.

Encouraged, Carver continued. "I . . . I did a computer search. There are only two Beauregard Morrows in the whole country." He paused to see how Marianna was taking this news, but she did not lift her face.

He waited several long moments.

"I think he may be the one in Kansas City, and we could. . . ."

"No." Her head was buried in her lap, and he could barely hear the words. "No, Carver."

Tony felt trapped. Here he was surrounded by fifteen smiling people, all facing each other in a sort of lopsided half circle. Hopefully Jake would cry in the middle of the meeting or service or whatever, and he could escape. But for now, an enraptured Dora had the baby in tow, and it didn't look like the kid was suffering any.

He'd been to church before — had some idea what it was all about. In fact he was a veteran of nineteen Easters. Mamita had insisted they go every spring, and after she died, Jack had kept this promise to her.

And so Tony and Jack had gone year after year, but never to the same place. They'd been inside cool, dark adobe Catholic churches, a clapboard-sided little Methodist church, two brick Presbyterian buildings, and four Lutheran edifices of various shapes and sizes. He'd heard great booming choirs, vast pipe organs, and tinny upright pianos with a single song leader. He'd always gone reluctantly — starched, pressed and slicked for the occasion — with a stern-faced Jack at his elbow.

Would they never stop gabbing? He thought people were supposed to shut up when they got inside a church.

But wait, things were starting to quiet down, because from behind him he could hear James' flute.

The music got closer and closer, and then he could see James walking slowly from the back bedroom, playing a simple lilting melody. Molly smoothed her green cotton dress and beamed at James, then turned to jab Paul with her elbow because he was tapping his foot too close to her new shoes.

Veda's ears stood at half-mast.

The haunting notes spilled over the group as they quieted. Slowly, James stepped behind and to the right of the little semi-circle and waited.

Hal, still seated, smiled broadly and began. "Let's pray a bit here to start." He cleared his throat a couple of times. Feet shuffled. Tony sweated. "Lord, you love us and you saved us, and when you died you brought us to Yourself. Now here we are with nothing to hide, and everything to give back to you."

More shuffling, some "Amens," and James lifting his flute to play again.

That's it!!? That's the whole prayer?? Tony sat dumbstruck.

"Who's carrying a load too heavy this morning?"

Silence. . . . More silence.

Hal didn't seem to care that the whole place was quiet as a tomb. Tony glanced quickly around him. Henry sat with arms folded across his chest, gazing at the ceiling. Jana pulled five-year-old Talia a little closer and seemed to be humming. Gil Longstreet, head bowed, covered his face with both hands.

Relaxed and unhurried, Hal put out the invitation again. "Jesus says we can give him our burdens and find comfort in walking in step with him. . . . Rest. . . . That's what you want, isn't it? Lean against him. When you're walking that close it's really hard to fall down. . . ."

Gil shuffled a little in his seat, then raised his hand. James began playing again, and it felt to Tony as if the notes dug through his heart and turned it inside out.

Once more he sat exposed.

James moved closer to Gil, then stopped a little way behind him and continued the music. Mel Brady got up quietly and moved behind Gil, laying his hands on the massive shoulders as the music continued.

"Would there be someone else who wants a prayer of rest?" Hal's voice was so soft Tony almost missed it. But whether it was the faint voice or the music or something he could not understand, Tony's arm raised ever so slightly, then shot down again. Sweat was pouring off his face now, and Will Johnson offered him a bright yellow bandanna.

James moved from behind Gil towards Tony.

By now the whole group was humming. What had begun as simple melody soon melted into harmony, as rich basses vibrated from Will, Hal and Henry, and poignant little sopranos piped from Molly and Talia.

When James lowered the wooden flute, Tony wiped his face with the bandanna, then sat limp and spent, wondering what had just happened.

But no one was looking at him. All had turned to stare at Jake, who was exploding happily into his morning call to nature.

He didn't care what Marianna said. Finally for once in his life Carver would do something right. He would not be like his father, bending the law until it broke. Marianna would come around. She'd see things his way. If he could just stand up and quit being a wimp.

He would make that phone call, explain it all to her while they drove west. At least she'd consented to that. Anything to get away, she'd said — just start driving.

———————————

Tony yelled over the din of the four-wheel-drive Polaris ATVs. "Why are the cows making so much racket?"

"Candy."

"What"? Maybe Henry hadn't heard him.

"Candy. Every time I put them in new pasture they think it's candy."

Two hundred cows and calves trailed behind the all-terrain-vehicles, bellowing and switching their tails. The shaggy Highlanders marshaled their young and lifted their broad faces heavenward, opening their mouths, rolling their eyes and sometimes erupting in sonorous blasts.

Henry swung his right leg over the ATV, slid off and walked along the single strand of conductive poly-wire to a red plastic handle. Grabbing the insulated lever, he unhooked it and pulled it back parallel with the rest of the electric fence. The cows edged forward, watching their gateway widen.

Tony parked his ATV under an ancient walnut tree. He swiveled in his seat and marveled at the long horns on two hundred shaggy heads, and how each cow miraculously dodged her neighbors. He'd hate to get tangled up in a free-for-all.

He got off the Polaris, picked up a couple of walnuts, and positioned himself near the gate, wanting to be helpful but without the faintest idea of what he was doing.

Henry yelled, waving wildly. "Stand back! Here they come!"

Suddenly, a mass of bovine bodies surged and shoved and jostled through the thirty-foot opening in one huge gentle stampede. Tony was so close he could see slobber looping in great strands from the lead cow. He marveled that the sixty or so calves squeezed right in there next to their trotting mothers without getting trampled, but he noted that the little black goat hung back judiciously, waiting for just the right moment to dart through the gate.

The cattle tossed their giant horns and moved purposefully into lush new pasture, fanning out over several acres. It wasn't long before they were tearing up huge mouthfuls of sweet grass and clover, as if they'd been standing right here in this pasture all day. The calves were old enough now for their own green lunch, their mothers' milk all but forgotten.

As suddenly as it had begun, the rumble of hooves stopped and only the gentle swishing of tails and munching of grass punctuated the crisp September day. Here and there an occasional bellow from a wandering cow recalled a misplaced calf.

Tony stared at the vegetation near the fence opening. In a fifty-foot swath not a blade of grass was standing upright, and all was thoroughly mixed with mud and manure.

"That will look brand new again in seven days. But I won't put those cows back in this paddock again for three weeks."

"Do you move them every day?"

"Every single day. Rain or shine."

Henry jammed his hands in his pockets and gazed over his cows. "Twenty-four paddocks, about ten acres each. When you do it this way it duplicates the way buffalo did it two hundred years ago. But if you let those cattle graze down a big pasture — even a pasture as big as three hundred acres where they're all spread out — they destroy it."

Henry folded his arms and smiled at a point in the distance. "This is what you call intensive grazing. It's healthier for the herd and the pasture both."

Tony opened his mouth to say something, but Henry pushed on. "Lots of folks think we should just let huge chunks of our world absolutely alone. They think that's the only way to make it perfect."

He paused and shook his head. "But it's a proven fact — we can make the land better by grazing it with cattle. Look at the weeds on the other side of that fence."

Tony could just see the vegetation at the edge of Pete Keidel's cornfield, where he'd struggled to bring Jake to safety two weeks before. The grass was gray-green, limp and overgrown with weeds.

As if reading his mind Henry said, "I test this soil for major nutrients and trace minerals every year." His arm swung in an arc over the pasture. "What you see on this side of the fence is a combination of intensive grazing and good mineral uptake in the grasses."

They stood silently side by side, enjoying the gentle swish of cow tails and the muted munching of grass.

Tony groped for something intelligent to say. "What do they do for water?"

"Some of the pastures have ponds or creek water. The rest I just tank." Henry got on his ATV again, whistling something from Beethoven's Ninth Symphony.

Tank? Tony scratched his head, then shrugged. This time he would not ask. There was only so much ignorance he was willing to spout in one day.

"I'm going to get Jake."

Henry turned sharply. "No. Do not bring him out here. These cows may be good-tempered, but there are too many things that could happen in a herd this size. No — you leave him with Molly."

Mile after mile the white Lexus followed the Platte River west through Nebraska. For a hundred and fifty miles the streambank meandered on their right as a sun-tinged plethora of cormorants, egrets and plovers glided gracefully in and out of their line of sight.

Marianna and Carver crossed the bridge at Maxwell, this time putting the river to their left, where a bright menagerie of water birds flitted, hovered and flopped into view.

First it was a pair of red-winged blackbirds, then three whooping cranes rose in heavy flight, nearly grazing their windshield. Thousands of geese honked and pecked their way through acres of corn awaiting the final harvest near the water's edge.

And for just a little while, they lost themselves in this long ribbon of fantasy land.

———————————

Jack was elated. He'd heard from Tony every night this week. They'd both been upbeat, avoiding the old pitfalls. And in three days he'd visit the farm again, this time to hear what Attorney Grace Longstreet had to say. Somehow it would work out. They'd be a family again.

His hopes soared. He'd untangled Beth from her missing-car alibis. Shannon Memorial was "using Danny for now but we'll hold Tony's job for him."

Now it was time to bring Tony back home.

Jack flexed his muscles.

———————————

Marianna had not come home last night, or the night before. None of her friends had seen her. Or, more accurately, none of her friends would tell Helene where she was. She could not — or would not — call Mayor Furman Adams, on the advice of her lawyer.

The carefully woven life of Helene Pardiac Morrow was unraveling, and no one was there to tie up the threads.

23

Henry Sebastian was transformed. In white shirt, blue striped tie and dark pants he looked more like an executive than a rancher. As he adjusted his tie in the mirror he caught Tony staring at him. Henry's eyes sparkled. "A man for all seasons — am I right?"

"You look great, dude."

"Well, this dude won't be out late. The cattlemen's meeting is in Rapid City and I plan to come home right after supper. You won't have to worry about anything except taking care of Jake."

Tony fidgeted. "Do you . . . want me to milk Sheilah?" He'd tried it once. The little goat had suffered in dignified silence.

Henry repressed a smile. "Molly will take care of her after school."

He gestured towards the kitchen. "There's plenty of milk in the refrigerator. Just don't forget to dilute it with water."

Henry stepped into his office to retrieve his billfold and a slip of paper. "I've moved the cattle to their pasture. Here is my cell phone number. Call if you need anything."

He headed for the door, then turned. "I'm only scheduled one time — for a speech on intensive grazing right before lunch."

He caught something in Tony's expression that troubled him. A flickering doubt? Fear?

He laid his huge gentle hand on Tony's shoulder and held his eye for a moment. "Please call if you need me."

Tony watched as the big rancher left the house whistling a tune from Beethoven or Albinoni or some strange guy. He watched Henry pause to stroke Veda, cupping her head in his hand. Whatever he said made her ears droop.

Then he got into his Silverado and slowly headed south on the tree-lined driveway.

———————————

The silence after Henry left was unsettling. Tony had always been surrounded by noise — his stereo, the clinks and bangs of the hospital's inner workings — and the chattering voices of co-workers, friends and pool hall regulars. Jake was asleep, and it was so absolutely quiet and empty that Tony was acutely aware of the beating of his own heart.

Outside, Veda lowered her head, then plopped to the ground. She heaved a big sigh and planted her whiskery face between her paws. Tony figured she'd ignore him the rest of the day.

Molly could be a jabbering little mina bird and Jake's cry was often annoying. But suddenly Tony yearned for those familiar sounds, for the happy chaos that had surrounded him for nearly three weeks. He walked into the bedroom to check on Jake. Even the baby's sleep was quiet for once, without the usual squeaks and burblings.

Outside, clouds lay in fluffy whipped cream sculptures, bunching up from the west. Soon they would blanket the sky. The sun glimmered weakly, submitting grudgingly to the drawing curtain of gray and white. Before the day was spent, it would rain.

Tony stepped out the back door. The late September air was heavy and still, smelling of sun-drenched grapes. Tomato vines lay in wild profusion against a flagstone walkway, surrounded by fragrant thyme, basil, peppermint and chives.

Crickets chirped in frantic concert, with the sure knowledge of the coming cold and the end of their lives.

Farther down the path, mammoth pumpkins were in their prime. Tony tried to lift one and gave it up. Behind them: beets, turnips, carrots and rutabagas stood with their tops in stately rows.

Henry kept a rich larder — daily he picked over his garden, deciding which ones to can, freeze, dry or store in the root cellar. And which ones to try on his guests. Inside of twenty days Tony had eaten more exotic stuff than he'd sampled in a lifetime. It spooked him that he was beginning to like it.

Tony munched a few cherry tomatoes, picked a handful of raspberries, and headed back to the house. He checked on Jake, then poked his head into Henry's office and eyed the computer. Henry had shown him the ranching software *Cow Sense,* and how each Highlander went through the computer system from conception to market.

Surely this "man for all seasons" was a sophisticated businessman. Tony figured he'd need at least five years of living in this house before he could begin to fathom the depths of Henry Sebastian.

Tony grabbed a magazine and plunked down in the sprawling leather chair by the fireplace. It was something about Jesus and the "Last Days." Well, he didn't want to think about the last days, or even the middle days or the first days. He'd done enough laboring over who he was, and he could never figure out where to go from here.

He slapped the magazine down and glanced at the stereo. Nope. He wasn't in the mood for Bach or Beethoven, either. Tony went down the hall again to check on the baby.

What was the matter with Jake? Why was he sleeping so late? Tony stared down at the bed for a long time, then he began rocking the little oaken fortress in gentle sweeps, hoping to stir up some action.

Jake wasn't the same shriveled puny infant he'd found behind the autoclaves five weeks ago. His face then had been a muddy purple. Now, although he was still a little on the thin side, there was a healthy glow to his honey brown skin.

On his head a puff of soft black hair pointed upwards. What would become of him? Would he have to give him up? Tony shoved the thought into the caverns of his mind and shivered. "God only knows," he whispered. And this time, he believed it.

Her nose was getting bigger. But so were the eyes. Now the head was shaking back and forth and the mouth was working furiously. *Smile, smile, smile. Do it, Jake, do it.* And Jake smiled. He clutched his hands and jerked one arm, then sent the blanket into a series of bumps while he worked his little legs. He would smile for Molly, over and over again, and never get tired of it.

Now Molly was swinging him back and forth, laughing and planting raspberries on his cheek. He twitched his hands, ready to reach up and touch her face, but somehow he couldn't move.

He'd try again. There! He did it! Up with the arm. Up with the eyelids.

Jake stared. *This isn't Molly. . . . It's the man with the bumpy arms!* He focused, trying to figure this out.

Tony was smiling.

So he would smile too.

Time to get up!!

Good. He's awake. Finally. Why should he think something was wrong with Jake? What could go wrong in a place like this? Mumbling a little jazz tune and weaving back and forth, Tony plucked Jake from the cradle and swung him around, then set him on a towel for a fast cleanup.

"What would you like for breakfast, Jake? Goat milk, goat milk — or goat milk?"

156

Now. What to do with Jake for the next couple of hours. Molly and Henry could always give some good diversion. But here he was on his own, in a big empty house on a vast lonely farm. He scooped up the baby and looked out the window. He could just see a clump of shaggy Highlanders as they crested the hill, occasionally moving their long horns from side to side and ambling in twos and threes towards the north. Henry had put them in the paddock closest to the house.

It wouldn't be far to walk out there and introduce Jake to all those four-footed friends while he and the baby stood safely behind the fence. He wouldn't even have to take the ATV — indeed he knew better than to put Jake in that rough little wooden basket over the front fenders.

"Jake! Ready for a hike, little guy?" Jake responded with a turtle face, then gripped Tony's calloused finger with his little fist.

"Hey, little turtle. Wanna go for a walk?" Tony dressed Jake with a ragged knit cap of Paul's and a tiny sweater of Molly's. They fit snugly over hand-me-down pajamas.

"Hey, buddy. Let's stop and see Carrot."

Now the white clouds from the west were edged with black, piling over themselves in a rush to hide the sun. Tony figured he'd just have time to walk to the pasture fence, let Jake see the cows, then head back to the house before the storm front swirled in.

He held Jake in his left arm and carried a small container of molasses-coated oats in the other. If the cows weren't at the fence-line, Tony planned to entice them by shaking his little bucket of sweet treats. He'd seen Henry rattle the bucket over the wire and *zoom* — a galloping herd of horned beasts would snort up from nowhere in just a few seconds.

Well, the beasts were not in sight now. Probably just over the north hill. He stopped for awhile under the walnut tree, listening to the crunch of green nuts under his boots. Then he secured Jake more tightly under his arm and walked towards the barbed wire. He leaned against the tension bar at the gate post, shaking the bucket.

Nothing. No cows. Jake wiggled in his arms.

"Hey, little buddy. They're out there. I know they're out there. We'll just have to wait." He shook the bucket again. In the silent morning it seemed as if the clouds were the ones making all the noise. A cool breeze freshened from the northwest.

Tony walked along the barbed wire towards the main pasture gate. This fence was not like the single strand of striped poly wire which Tony had seen Henry open between the two paddocks last week. This was what Henry called the line fence — four strands of tightly stretched barbed wire surrounding the entire two hundred and eighty acres of pasture.

The gate, too, was made of four strands of barbed wire twenty feet long. Each wire had been wrapped around a solid fence post on one side, then stretched tightly to a vertical hardwood four-by-four on the other side.

Tony sized it up. He saw how the simple tensioning device kept the gate wires stretched tight as piano strings. To close the gate, you'd first put that vertical four-by-four inside a heavy wire loop near the ground.

At the top, a two-foot oak lever was connected to the anchor post by a heavy wire. You'd bring the lever behind the vertical bar, pull it to make the four-strand gate tight, and lock the lever in place with the smaller wire loop at the top.

Like wrestling someone's neck into an armlock. Wonder what farmer thought of this first.

Tony laughed aloud. "One thing for sure — I'm not dragging us under a fence like we did a few weeks ago."

Tony shifted Jake to his left arm. With his right hand he tested the tension on the top wire loop which secured the square-ended locking bar. The loop was just an inch from the end of the bar, in a well-worn groove.

Tony laughed. "Hey, Little Buddy, quit your squirmin'! Let's have some fun. Just watch your Uncle Tony the cowboy!"

Jake caught the excitement and began kicking his legs.

Tony worked to free the locking wire. The tension was so tight he couldn't slide it off with his right hand. It was probably easy for Henry. But then, Henry was strong as a bull. Tony braced himself and pushed harder.

He felt it first as it grazed his chest — then a dull thwang like the sound of a baseball bat hitting the dirt. Barbed wire screeched beneath staples as the loop was finally set free from its groove, turning the stout tension bar into a vicious weapon.

Tony saw three things in that first quarter second: Jake was face-down on the grass, the gate was wide open, and the cows had finally come thundering over the hill.

24

"**J**ake. . . . *JAKE!*" Tony screamed the name over and over as he grabbed the baby and half-crawled, half-ran, stumbling and scrabbling his way along the fenceline.

No time to close the gate. No time for anything.

His words came in gasps. "Oh Jake, Jake. . . . I'm sorry, I'm sorry!"

Behind him, a boiling tide of shaggy cows and their gangly calves shoved and bellowed their way through the fifty-foot gap, horns glistening under the last rays of sunlight.

Tony could feel the body heat and their steamy breath as he sheltered Jake away from the herd and sprinted with his precious bundle towards the house.

As Tony ran, he plucked at hope, weaving it in and out of his frantic thoughts. *Jake's clothes were bulky. It wasn't such a long fall. The grass was soft.* Tony's lungs began to burn as he willed one leg in front of the other.

Maybe Jake wasn't too bad off. He was wailing a muffled choking cry against Tony's chest, but surely he'd be okay if they could just get to the house.

He felt the concentrated energy of the herd behind him. But there was nothing he could do to stop the thundering tide. They were out in the open. Two hundred horned beasts loose in the woods, on the road, in the park. He couldn't bear to think about it.

Suddenly, off his right shoulder, he saw a flash of black as Veda exploded behind him with savage fury. With unholy yowls and yips she snapped at legs, rumps and tails. The huge whiskery dog, shoulders bristling, was everywhere at once.

Slowly the vast horned army retreated in confusion. Some of the cows stood stubbornly, heads lowered, feet stiffly apart, their slobber drooling in ropes. But Veda's swift aim was always at their back legs, where the lumbering bovines were slow to focus.

Soon they could no longer function as a herd, and reluctantly they began retreating to the other side of the fence, bawling in protest. Only a few stragglers headed for the woods.

"Oh Jake, Jake. Sweet Jake. Look at me, Baby!" Tony stopped running and held the little guy in front of him, hands trembling violently. Then he saw it — blood cascading down the tiny face. Jake was screaming now, and choking as the red stream trickled into his mouth.

"Where. . . . *Wha. . .*?"

In a swift flash of horror he remembered now — the stick, the stout tension stick with its rough end — had sliced across Jake's forehead and tumbled him to the ground. Frantically, Tony pulled the little cap lower, hoping to staunch the flow.

For as long as he lived he would never forget this macabre sight — the dark blue stocking cap against that bright red blood.

Why, why why! Why didn't I just stay in the house! Why'd I have to be the big macho cowboy. "Oh, my God, my God!" Tony cried. It was a frantic prayer as he fled for the house — the first raindrops splattering his face.

He stole a last helpless look at Veda, who had planted herself with curled upper lip into the center of the churned-up gateway. The giant dog turned her head towards the retreating pair.

And for just a moment Tony was sure that snarling mouth was meant just for him.

Hands slippery with blood, Tony dialed Dora and held the portable phone between shoulder and ear while he fumbled frantically in Henry's medicine closet for herbs, bandages, ointments, *anything*! On the sofa, Jake howled in angry guttural rasps.

No answer at Dora's.

Henry! Where's that cell number! What'd I do with it! No! It was already eleven-thirty. Henry was giving his speech!

Stop the bleeding. Stop. Yes. What'd they say in health class. Pressure. Okay. Okay. Pressure. Here, behind those jars of herbs, the big bandages. Tony's hands were shaking so hard he could barely open the package.

"Jake, Jake. . . . Sshh . . . shh." Holding a bandage against the bloody head, Tony looked around wildly for some kind of fastener. Then he glanced down. The bandage was already soaked, and behind it, an ugly open gash. Dear God, he'd have to do something fast. Grabbing two more bandages he held them both to Jake's head, then pulled the blood-soaked cap down over them and raced into the kitchen, groping in Henry's cupboards and drawers.

There! Tony fastened the whole thing — cap and bandages — with duct tape.

He scooped up Jake and ran for the door.

Henry's pickup. In the shed. *Hurry. Hurry.*

"Jake! Jake! We'll fix it. We'll fix it. We've *got* to. . . . Just hang in there!"

The old pickup. No seat belts, no power brakes, and a jagged gaping hole in the floor. Tony cranked and cranked, holding the key in a vise grip. Finally it sputtered to life, just as the storm unleashed its fury. Fine sifted dust rose in a cloud from the earthen floor, then mixed with rain in a splatter of mud as the '76 Dodge roared out of the machine shed.

Somehow he'd get to Colchester's main drag. "The town is south, then east," was all Henry had told him. Country roads dipped and curved endlessly as huge sheets of rain pummeled the pickup.

Jake had stopped wailing. He moaned pitifully inside a makeshift mound of rags and tarps.

The rain trickled in tiny streams inside the door, blending with watery mud that sprayed up from a jagged hole in the floorboard.

Tony looked at Jake again and his stomach lurched. Maybe the bleeding had slowed, but the gory little bundle at his side was a mass of smeared blood.

Tony glanced at his own sticky hands on the steering wheel. "Jesus, it's just you and me and Jake now. If you really do keep people from falling down like Hal said, I need a big helping hand, okay?"

Maybe, just maybe, there was a bit of peace seeping into the cab along with the rain. And just ahead — the streets of Colchester.

It was a weird way to enter a hospital, but he was desperate. "Ring buzzer for entrance," read the sign on a huge aluminum cargo door. Slowly the metal barrier lifted and Tony drove straight into a lighted concrete cavern, honking his horn.

Immediately he was surrounded by a swarm of paramedics and nurses, opening his door, helping him out, grabbing the baby, rushing him into the emergency room.

"Tell me what happened." A brisk young woman grabbed Tony's arm.

"I, I don't know. I mean I. . . . The fence — that stick on the fence. I was just going to show Jake the cows and . . . and when I opened the gate, the stick flew out and hit him." His throat was thick with grief. "I didn't mean to. I didn't mean to."

She nodded and pointed to a little room across the hall. "Please wait there. I'll be back in just a minute."

"No! I've gotta be with Jake! He's scared. Don't take him away!"

Two medics suddenly materialized, gently but firmly propelling Tony away from the emergency cubicle. "We can work better if you wait in here, Sir."

The young woman returned with a clipboard and pen. "Mr. . . ?"

"Ko . . . Kowalski."

"Mr. Kowalski, we'll need some information. They might even be finished with Jake by the time you fill out these forms. Then you can see him. Just fill in this part, under 'MINOR.'" She smiled briefly, then left.

Tony bent his head down to his knees. A numb blankness overwhelmed him like a drug. This was not real. It could not be real. From his throat came a single broken sob, animal-like and helpless. Slowly he raised his head and wiped his face, leaving smeary tracks of blood and dirt. He looked at the clipboard.

"NAME," it seemed to shout at him. "FIRST NAME."

"Jake."

"LAST NAME."

"None."

What was he doing! What kind of stupid report was he making! A sudden panic gripped him and he read further.

"NAME OF PARENT OR GUARDIAN." All the indecision and running of the last five weeks now culminated in that single phrase. He would have to declare what he knew about Jake.

He would have to separate himself from Jake on paper, "where it counts."

He crossed out the word "parent" and wrote "unknown." Then, after the word "guardian," he wrote "Antonio Kowalski."

"ADDRESS!" Why were all the questions screaming at him? What was Henry's address anyway? Well, he'd put his Cedar Bend address. No! That apartment was destroyed. And — he was shocked and ashamed to admit — he did not even know his father's new street number.

Father! He would call his father. Sudden relief filled him, unlike any comfort he had ever known. His father. . . . His father would know what to do.

25

Brian Todd McGinnis stood by the draped window in the Pediatric Intensive Care Unit, clipboard in hand.

In the metal crib next to him Jake stirred in troubled sleep, his tiny head swathed in bandages. The infant shirt from the hospital nursery covered his arms to the elbow. His hands clutched and unclutched, and occasionally the bandaged head would jerk to one side as a frown wrinkled his face. The gash on his forehead had taken fifteen stitches. A long cut for one so young, but at least there was no skull fracture.

Dr. McGinnis scowled at the report in his hand, where Melly Ferguson had written, "Accident with stick on barbed wire fence."

Accident with stick. During his residency he'd worked in the emergency room at Springfield General. He'd also been head of Emergency here at Dover County Hospital for nearly a year, and this was the first time he'd seen an "accident" with a stick. Sticks, clubs, rolling pins — call them what you want — were generally for hitting people. And he'd seen plenty of those reports.

Then, there was that barely visible two-inch scar on Jake's lower arm. He had missed it while working on the forehead. But once Jake was out of danger, cleaned and bandaged and finished with his X-rays, Brian had looked carefully at Jake's tiny frame, hunting for clues.

He'd been schooled very carefully, in those "mandatory-report" seminars, to note any signs of physical abuse. And he, Brian Todd McGinnis, M.D., was an official "mandatory reporter," bound by law to report all things suspicious.

Something else troubled him too. "Date of birth August 17," was the information given by his so-called guardian. Well, here it was September 21, and this baby was seven pounds, two ounces.

Brian quickly calculated the information he'd just gleaned from a pediatric nurse. If he figured very conservatively that the baby was as small as six pounds at birth — then lost a few ounces at first as they all did — that baby should have begun gaining four to seven ounces every week after the first ten days.

"Hmmm," he mumbled. "Five weeks old. Should be seven and a half or eight, even nine pounds by now. "Could have been a preemie. Maybe not."

Brian scrawled a quick reminder to himself on the clipboard: "Formula? Diet?" The doctor paused, pencil in hand, as he studied Jake one more time.

Then he jotted, "Check S. Mem. birth records."

Somehow Tony had managed to clean up a little with the soap dispenser in the men's room and twenty or thirty paper towels. One of the paramedics had given him a pair of green scrubs and now it was only his blood-encrusted work boots that gave him away.

They had let him see Jake, "but only for a moment so he can rest." Odd, that a loved one standing quietly by a bedside would somehow disturb sleep.

Tony had been acutely aware of the doctor's assessment of him as he stood by the crib. Jake had looked so tiny and vulnerable against the sterile sheets. The top of his head — even the little black puff of hair — was bound in bandages.

Did McGinnis think Tony was the cause of all this misery?

He had gazed in anguish at the sleeping baby. This was his son, he finally realized. Why did he have to be the one who hurt him! He would give his life to change what had happened today.

Now Tony slumped on a dark purple sofa in the hallway by the elevator, staring out the window. Minute after minute he sat in an agony of waiting. Gradually he became aware of the throbbing pain in his chest.

He rubbed his right hand over his heart, remembering the "thwang" as the wire released. He felt a long, swelling tenderness across his rib cage, where the hefty stick had done its first damage.

Tony's stomach lurched. He would gladly have offered his own body to stop that wooden stick dead in its tracks.

A quick tight squeeze on the back of his neck told him all he needed to know. "Dad!" Their embrace was tightly scripted and unspoken — fierce, almost painful.

"Son. Oh, my son."

No condemnation, no questions. They stood awkwardly by the window, each struggling with his emotions as they watched nurses and visitors on the sidewalk below.

"Do you have a court order?" The mellow voice of Taweeka Johnson at Shannon Memorial rippled over the phone.

Dr. McGinnis bristled. *Drat.* He was hoping to bluff his way around the HIPPA privacy laws. "Look. Can't you just tell me whether there were any boys delivered at Shannon about August seventeenth?"

There was a short pause. "Wait a minute please. Brian could hear the tippy-tap of the computer keyboard. "There were no boys born here on August sixteenth, seventeenth or eighteenth. And that's as much as I can tell you."

There was a pause as Brian McGinnis planned his next move. "Mmm. Okay. Please transfer me to the Maternity wing."

A click, a blank spot, a crisp tight voice. "Maternity."

"This is Dr. McGinnis at Dover. Who is your Chief of Obstetrics? I'd like to speak with him. Yes. Okay. Right. I've got the number. But when you see him, please have him call. It's urgent."

Nurse Otten repositioned her little stiff hat with one hand while she wrote with the other, "Quaid — McGinnis @ Dover. ~~Please~~ must call."

Brian McGinnis slumped a little in his desk chair, lips pursed, hands tented in front of his face.

He could never remember a case so straightforward. First, there was that wild-eyed "Tony" who claimed to be a guardian but didn't know the names of the baby's parents, and couldn't even give his own address. Worse, the guy kept contradicting his story.

Most likely on drugs.

Maybe even a kidnapping charge here.

And what about the vehicle Tony was driving? He'd heard the paramedics snickering about it — an old relic of a pickup, no seat belts, hole in the floor. No license plate. Dr. McGinnis straightened and walked to his file cabinet. He pulled open the drawer, located the folder, and lifted out a white form.

"Colchester Police."

"This is Dr. Brian McGinnis at Dover County. I've just put in a call to DHS concerning a child in imminent danger. We need intervention. Now."

"What have you got?"

"Well, for starters there's an injured baby and a teenager who can't explain how he came into possession of the child." McGinnis tapped his pencil against the desk. "Highly suspicious, in my book."

"Right. We'll send someone over. Just fax the medical report."

"Done. Five minutes ago."

Jake opened his eyes. He could not see much in this dim light. He seemed to be shrouded with shadows. And who was that looking at him? There was hair under the man's nose but he did not smile like the other man with the bushy mouth. No, he was frowning. Jake did not like that.

He could feel something numb and tight whenever he tried to move his head. Sharp air tickled his nose and made him sneeze. He turned his head a little, trying to find the girl with the happy mouth or the man with the bumpy arms.

Would someone lift him and press him into a soft thumpy warmth? Maybe if he cried, someone he loved would come. . . .

Lieutenant Jeffrey Sprague reached across his desk for the single white sheet. "Thanks, Scott." Then he swung back in his chair to scan the faxed report. *Rats. Not another child abuse case. I hate those.* He skimmed down the page. Antonio Kowalski, Guardian . . . "Jake" . . . blow to the head . . . previous suspected abuse . . . request immediate intervention. . . .

Sprague grabbed his keys and strode out the door with no comment to the trio in the outer office.

Jack walked quickly towards Lieutenant Sprague. He was beaming. "Jeff! I haven't seen you in ages. Man, we could use a friend right now. What. . . ." He reached out his hand, then let it fall slowly back to his side. Jeff stood with ashen face, arms crossed, staring at Tony.

"Is this your son?"

"Uh sure, yeah. . . . Tony, this is Lieutenant Jeff Sprague. We shared some cases together a couple of years ago. Jeff, this is Tony."

Jeff nodded quickly towards the boy, his face grim. "A word with you in private, Jack."

Tony watched as the two men walked down the hall, heads bent. He was having trouble processing the day's surreal events. His mind was about one hour behind everything that had happened so far, and this encounter with a Colchester cop was no exception. His brain and his emotions were on overload, and the only thing he knew for sure was that he was not ready for more trouble. He bent his head towards his knees and locked his hands behind his neck.

Sprague handed Jack the Temporary Removal Order. "We've just processed this."

Jack scanned the page, then lifted his face slowly in disbelief and horror. Jack had seen plenty of these orders, and he knew they could not be countermanded without a hearing. The word of the physician as "mandatory reporter" carried more weight than he wanted to think about right now. Getting Tony untangled from this mess could be a long, tortuous process.

Jeff felt the anguish. How many times had he knocked on a door to inform parents they'd lost a child, to tell a man he'd lost his wife. Well, this was no different. Even if Tony was proven innocent he would probably lose this baby — or at best suffer six months to a year slogging through Juvenile Court and the Department of Human Services. He reached out a hand and rested it on Jack's shoulder.

His voice was low and flat. "I'm . . . I'm sorry. As soon as Jake is discharged, they'll put him in foster care."

There was a long pause.

Lieutenant Sprague could hardly force himself to say the next words. "The baby isn't the only one involved with the law. We'd like Tony to come down to the station. Voluntarily — for questioning. It could go much better with him later if he does."

Jeff wiped one hand across his eyes. "Jack, look, this is just for questioning. You know how these things go."

"Yes, I know how these things go." An awkward pause. "What kinds of things are you thinking about here, Jeff?"

"You know I'm not supposed to say anything."

"I know." The two men stood side by side, staring at the floor — at the walls — looking at anything but each other.

Jeff hesitated, then began quietly: "Okay. Let's just suppose someone in this county came in from another county — or even from out of state — with a . . ."

He cleared his throat. "With a . . . stolen child."

"How can you steal a child who's been left to die?" Neither of them had seen Tony, who had slipped quietly behind his father.

26

The clerk at Elko County's License Bureau straightened her glasses and stole a quick look over the computer screen. She'd been uneasy for the last hour, directing covert glances at the middle-aged gentleman standing silently in the foyer, hugging the wall like a shadow.

Now there was this new pair of marriage license applicants coming through the glass doors.

Hester Nemeier had been at the same job for twenty-three years, and it was second nature for her to size up a couple at first glance. Tall and standing just a little too straight, the prospective groom held tightly to the girl's elbow.

Spoiled, rich Yuppie. Doesn't know the first thing about marriage. Her practiced glance took in the small timid girl at his side. *Can't be a day over fifteen.*

Hester sighed. She was the only one at the counter today, so she'd have to be the one to tell them — yes, Nevada law was possibly the most lenient in the nation, but it didn't hold kindly to hitching up little girls with men old enough to be their uncles or fathers.

"Age?"

"Twenty-four." Carver slid his drivers license across the counter in one swift move.

Hester cleared her throat, lowered her glasses, and looked

directly at Marianna. "Age?"

"I'm . . . almost seventeen."

Hester's face softened. "That would make you sixteen, Honey. Below the legal age. Need to be eighteen in this state . . . unless you have parental permission."

"I . . . don't know. . . . I . . . ."

"She does." The shadowy man near the wall had moved through the double doors, emerging silently from behind the couple.

Marianna drew in a sharp breath and moved closer to Carver. She began shivering violently.

"And you are. . . ?" Hester was plenty used to drama in her little licensing office, but this was something new.

"I'm her father."

Marianna buried her face in Carver's shirt and began sobbing. "I asked you not to. I told you not to."

"Sh-h-h-h. Sh-h-h-h. He wanted to come, Marianna. And it's just for now . . . just for the paperwork."

Beauregard Morrow stood uncertainly, clutching a gray, creased envelope. He lifted his arm slightly, hand extended — then let it drop. He turned towards Carver and fixed him with pale, tired eyes. "Take care of her. That's all I ask. Just . . . take care of her."

He jammed the envelope into the dark hand that held his little girl. "I'll be outside in the hall." He left as silently as he had come.

Henry wasn't used to going seventy-five. But here he was, streaking down the wet county roads in his Silverado, negotiating hairpin turns like a NASCAR driver.

Dora had called.

"Dad. Don't go to Colchester. Jake and Tony are okay. Please . . . come straight home. Veda's got most of the cattle back in the pasture, but there must be about twenty of them roaming the park. I've

176

called the ranger." Henry heard just a whisper of a broken sob. "I've got to clean up the mess before Molly gets here. She mustn't know about this. Not yet. I'm praying, Dad. I'm praying."

Thank God she'd stopped by the house and seen the blood before Molly arrived. Calmly she'd begun making calls, finally tracing Tony to the hospital. Bless her, thought Henry. She had Gloria's brains.

What a rotten day. Christa Jamison shoved her purse and brief case under the rest room sink, then ran water over a paper towel and patted her sweaty face, brushing limp tendrils of brown hair away from her neck. From the time she'd finally plopped into her chair at the Dover County Department of Human Services that morning the phone had not stopped ringing — everyone needed a Child Protective Investigator and they needed one right *now*!

No time for lunch — just a stale granola bar washed down with juice from the pop machine. Now, when she's just an hour away from going home to who-knows-what other crisis, here comes this urgent call from the county hospital.

Christa jammed her purse into the bulging brief case and hefted it to her shoulder. Another cut up, damaged, god-forsaken child. She'd have to quit soon, or drop in her tracks from a broken heart.

Child endangerment! Child abuse! Child hurting! Dropping! Breaking! Stupid, stupid, stupid! Tony had slammed the dreaded words through his mind all afternoon, making up new ones to torment himself.

There was a kind of numb safety in this constant mental scourging. But he'd repeated the words inside his head so many times he was beginning to believe them.

Right here in this windowless little interrogation room with the low ceiling and the acrid smell of stale cigarettes was probably where he really belonged. There was no way he could make anyone believe him — that he'd "found" a baby in the hospital and with the best of intentions had kept it a secret from everyone.

Lieutenant Jeff Sprague and Captain Ward Putnam had drilled him with the same simple questions for over two hours. "Where did you get the baby. . . . Why did you take him. . . . Who helped you. . . . Where are the parents. . . ."

And every time Tony answered, he saw a little more clearly how guilty he must look. And, God help him, he was probably making Beth, Randy and his father look guilty too. In another room they had questioned Jack. Tony just hoped their stories matched.

But what could they say that would make any sense? Was he guilty, after all?

He hoped Grace Longstreet would come. Maybe Henry would get home in time to call her. Tony had left a message on the ranch phone.

Please come, Grace. He quietly mouthed the words as he slumped in his chair. *Grace, grace, grace!* Henry had talked about grace, even before he'd introduced him to the family attorney. He'd said grace was God's way of wiping out sin, especially when we did not deserve it.

Well, it wasn't working. The more he thought about the trip to the police station and this suffocating little room, the more he was sure God would never wipe out that terrible deed at the cattle gate. Henry had warned him twice about the danger.

And he hadn't listened.

"Your attorney is here." Lieutenant Sprague and Captain Putnam stood. Jeff shuffled papers, scooped up the mini recorder and clipped his pen into a pocket. Sprague motioned to Tony. "We'll give you some time alone."

Tony was facing the wall when he sensed a shadow drifting across his side of the table. A slight whiffling of aluminum chair legs against the glued-down carpet — a soft fluttering of papers against the table. Then a touch on his shoulder so light that it might not have been.

"This is a rough day for you, isn't it."

Tony turned towards the voice. He nodded, then slowly stood to hold her chair. "Mrs. . . . Longstreet."

"Please. Call me Grace." She busied herself with the worn, pliable attache case at her feet, shifting papers, setting out two pencils and a tape recorder, folding back the first sheet on a plump tablet.

"You've already told me some of your story, Tony. But I want you to start from the beginning. Tell me everything, as if I had never heard it." She paused, pencil in the air. "And when we're finished here, we can both talk to the DHS investigator."

———————

"We can't hold him. Not without a formal charge, and I don't think we can come up with one in the twenty-two hours we've got left. Sheesh, what a mess. If he's telling the truth we're dealing with at least three counties here. But if he's not — maybe it's much bigger than that. We could be talking about crossing a state line."

"Lots of state lines."

"Maybe drugs."

"Right now I'd say Peterman's thinking about a kidnapping charge."

"Nah. That wouldn't fit. There wasn't any ransom. More like child stealing."

"Either way, we're talking serious time. Peterman's pressing hard. Wants this investigation tight and clean."

There was an uncomfortable silence. Everyone remembered County Attorney Barry Peterman's little girl, abducted five years earlier.

"Yeah. Captain Putnam's handing this over to Roy and Sean. The FBI regional director — Currie — she's coming down from Riverside tomorrow. Cedar Bend's in this too. Who knows — maybe it really could have started there, like Tony said."

"If the FBI's involved, it'll be Currie's show."

"Who's checking the so-called accident site at that rancher-what's-his-name's place?"

"Sean and Roy. They're on it."

––––––––––––––––––––

"What . . . what does that mean?" Tony licked his lips.

"It means . . . it means they'll have to keep Jake in foster care until they've wrapped up this investigation.

"How . . . how long . . . would that be?"

Grace shifted uneasily. "These things take time, Tony."

He swallowed hard, color draining from his face. "How long?"

"Maybe a month. Two months."

"Two months!" Tony clamped his hands on the edge of the table. "But . . . *Jake.* I can't go that long without seeing Jake! Where is he! who's taking care of him!"

A hard panic, strong as steel, was pulling all the breath out of his body. "Jake won't make it if they take him away now. They can't do that! They *can't.*"

Tony got up and pounded his fists against the wall. Sprague poked his head in the doorway, but Grace shook her head, silently thankful she hadn't said what she really feared — it could take as long as six months.

"Sit down, Tony." She paused, then reached out both hands and laid them on his arms. "Tony, look at me."

She waited while he fixed dull eyes on her face. "Do you remember what you saw at Henry's house a couple of Sundays ago? Did you see those men and women and children in the circle? Fifteen people."

She gripped his arms more tightly. "But you didn't see just fifteen people. What you saw was one body. A body of believers. And let me tell you — something happens when fifteen believers ask God for a miracle. It's dark now for you. Real dark. But you just keep lifting your eyes, Tony, and expecting God to do something."

She waited a long moment, staring at him, unblinking. "Because, Tony, He loves Jake more than we can ever imagine, and He *will* do something. All you have to do is wait."

Tony closed his eyes. His father had told him so many lifetimes ago that taking care of Jake could be the hardest thing he would ever do.

His father was wrong.

Christa Jamison was not one to swear. But oh, how she wanted to vent with something. At home they'd encouraged the kids to make up ditzy words to let off steam. Nine-year-old Farley Jamison often yelled "Mushburger," while four-year-old Katie erupted from time to time with "Pickle pots!" Their father, not to be outdone, would blast out something that sounded suspiciously like the real thing.

Well, none of those crazy words was strong enough for the report Christa was holding in front of her. She searched her mind for a good one, then finally just lowered her head and let go with a few tears of frustration and fatigue.

"You okay?" Dr. McGinnis poked his head into the tiny office where Christa had spread her papers.

"Yeah, yeah. I'm gonna be." She wiped her eyes and straightened. "Do you have a few minutes? Tell me what you know. And after this, I'll run over to the Police Department and see young Mister Kowalski."

Christa recovered herself and smoothed down her jacket.

Laptop open, she gave Todd her full attention.

He'd rounded up illegal immigrants, drug smugglers — even a counterfeit gang. But these shabby beasts were something else again. Jack would have to quit apologizing for his clumsy ineptness and go back to the house. Worse, he'd been told with direct firmness that the ranger and Will and Henry would bring in the cattle while Veda hunted for stragglers.

Now he leaned against the open door frame, sipping coffee and staring blankly at the wet garden. Faintly from the woods he heard cattle lowing and an occasional shout of triumph.

Never had time been so hard to kill. A man of simple purpose, Jack was not used to waiting. If there was a crime, he'd investigate. If physically threatened he could disable his attacker with one powerful motion.

But waiting? Jack wasn't sure he could do it, when every fiber of his being ached for his son and screamed for action.

In the next room they shuffled in quietly. Jack did not hear them until they were all seated — on the floor, on the chairs, on the hearth.

"You must be Tony's father." A tall lanky man held Jack's arm in a firm clasp. "I'm Hal, this is James, Dora, Gil. . . ." He continued around the little circle.

"And this is Molly." He motioned to the small dark-haired girl huddled next to Talia. "She and Tony are buddies."

After a whispered prodding, Molly walked towards Jack, lifted up her solemn face and extended her hand.

He smiled down at her. "Thank you for being Tony's friend," he began. Molly opened her mouth to answer, then suddenly burst into tears and ran back to Talia.

Hal steered Jack towards the kitchen. "It's been hardest on that little one. At first we tried to keep this from her but in the end we knew it wasn't right to stop her from praying with us. We can all take a lesson from her simple faith. Possibly she's the strongest believer in this entire circle."

Jack smiled grimly as he came back to the group and sat gingerly on the edge of a ladderback chair. *Certainly stronger than I am.*

"Yes, Judge, I know it's after five o'clock." Christa struggled to keep her voice even. No sense riling the one person who could be her best friend in this tangled mess. "This is high priority. We need a foster care placement order right now. Yes. . . . Yes, tonight. Just call over to the hospital and ask for Dr. McGinnis. And thank you. Thank you very much!"

Christa hung up the phone, massaged the back of her neck and exhaled heavily. Remarkable. She'd found a Juvenile Court judge who'd consented to verbalizing the placement order right at closing time. Maybe there was a God.

"Oh my." Carrie Johnson fumbled with the kitchen chair and thumped down heavily. "Tomorrow?" She pulled her stringed pencil towards her. "Well, I don't have much time to think about this, do I."

She paused to wipe her face with a dish towel. "I know we'd asked for a bit of a break last year after Will's surgery. Yes, yes. . . . He's fine now." Carrie paused a few moments, thinking it through.

Then she straightened slowly and pulled herself tall in the chair. "Of course, Miz Jamison. Yes, of course we'll take him." She fumbled to hold the paper straight. "Yes. Tomorrow. Three O'clock. Uh huh. At the hospital. I can speak for Will. He'll be all right with this. Yes, we . . . we still have Danny's car seat."

Carrie slumped and folded her arms across her chest, shaking her head slowly from side to side. "Mercy, mercy! A baby again. All that walking and bouncing around in the middle of the night. Lord, you got to help us with this one!"

She labored up the stairs of the old farmhouse and opened the door to the small bedroom. It had not changed since Danny. The narrow white dresser, the old maple crib and the starched and faded yellow curtains looked so patient in the early evening light, as if waiting for someone to return. Hugging the mattress was the snowy sheet with its tiny gold and green teddy bears, put on fresh before bedtime nearly two years ago.

But Danny had not returned to his bed that night. He was taken from Carrie and Will's home long before evening had settled over the farmhouse. "Back to his mother," they'd said, "where he belongs." Danny was six months old when Carrie and Will said their last goodbyes. He never made it to his first birthday.

Carrie closed the door softly, then leaned heavily against the door frame. "Lord, I need a *lot* of mercy!"

They'd let him off by the gate. Good. The long walk through the trees would give Tony time to think.

But as he picked his way over the gravel he felt like a trespasser. Soon, the urge to turn around and run was overwhelming.

The outer edge of the driveway was filled with cars and there was no way he'd go in that house to a church service or whatever else was going on. Maybe he could stay in the barn until everyone had gone home. He raised the latch on one of the double doors and silently pushed it open a few feet.

Inside the barn he could hear the whiff and thunk of ropes and harness against wood, and a faint rendering of Beethoven's Ninth

Symphony. *Henry!* This was the last person he wanted to see.

Tony backed out quietly, hand on the door, ready to pull it closed behind him. Maybe he'd walk in the woods awhile. Just so he wouldn't have to explain himself. But a low growl announced his presence, and Veda's collar tags clinked as she moved forward to investigate Tony's purpose.

Henry did not turn around or straighten from his work. "We got the cows out of the woods. They're back where they belong." There was a pause. "Carrot's in the pasture too, along with her colt." He stopped to hang some chains against the wall. "They no longer need the protection of this stall."

Tony's jaw worked convulsively and tears coursed down his cheeks. "I . . . I'm sorry, Henry. I . . . didn't mean to bring all this junk down on you."

Henry leaned a pitchfork against the rough planks and lowered himself onto a bale of straw.

"God gave you a job to do. . . ."

"And I messed it up, big time."

"I guess that would be true."

Tony lowered his head.

"But just because you slipped up doesn't mean God doesn't care about you anymore."

Tony sat staring at the dirt floor. There was a long silence.

Henry's eyes softened. "It doesn't mean I've stopped caring for you either."

Tony lifted his eyes, met Henry's and lowered them again. He shook his head slowly. "It's no good, Henry. It's too big a mess. There's nothing anybody can do now."

"There was another man in trouble once — just like you." Henry flicked a clod of manure off his boot with a stick.

Tony didn't answer.

"It was someone who lived a long time ago. He stole somebody — kind of like you're suspected of doing."

"A baby?"

"A woman."

Tony lowered himself against the rough-hewn wall and rested his hands on his knees. "You mean like kidnapping?"

"I mean like adultery."

Tony's eyes flashed. "Look — I never touched Jake's mother. Never even met her!" His face tightened and he jutted out his chin. Veda rumbled softly in her throat.

Henry put out a hand, palm forward. "No, no. I don't mean you did the same thing. But all such things — whether big or small — what you did and what that man did — are acts against God's loving plan for us."

Tony's frown had eased but there was a glint of defiance in his eyes.

Henry rubbed his hands together slowly. "Look. Today when I raced home in the Silverado, I cut off a driver — made her pull off the road."

His musical voice was tense now. "That's just one tiny example of things I've done wrong or thought of doing wrong ever since I was a little boy. I could name you a thousand ways I've 'messed up' as you say — in God's sight — and not even begin to cover the list."

He relaxed, leaned against the wall. "And God loves me just as much today as he has for more than seventy years."

Tony kept his mouth shut, his body tense. Where was Henry going with this?

"Anyway, that's not all this man did."

Tony lifted his head.

"He killed the woman's husband to cover his tracks."

Tony sat with his mouth open. This was way out of his league.

"What do you think God thought of him then?"

"I . . . suppose he didn't want much to do with him after that."

"Well. . . ." Henry cleared his throat. "God had a great deal to do with King David — that was his name. In fact, a long time after the king died, God talked about David's heart. You can read about it in the Book of Kings."

There was a vast silence. Veda lowered her head down to her paws, wrinkling her eyebrows from side to side as she looked first at Henry and then at Tony.

"God knew that down deep, David's heart was devoted to him — in fact God even said it was 'perfect' — the same as it had been from the time David was seventeen years old."

Tony waited.

"He said David's heart. . . ." Henry paused, a catch in his throat. "Was like God's own heart."

"So David was . . . just like God?"

"No. What I mean is that God gave a full measure of forgiveness to those who were willing to humble themselves and admit they were wrong. He promised to erase any wrong-doing so that David's heart would become perfect in God's sight."

Henry stopped talking — looked at his feet. Tony thought maybe he was finished.

Henry cleared his throat and wiped one beefy hand across his eyes. "And David, well, he was 'a man after God's own heart' because he always wanted so badly to do whatever it took to get close to God again — every time he did something wrong."

There was a soft crunch of gravel, then Jack stepped into the circle of light near the barn door. He cleared his throat. "They sent me out here to see if you were back, Tony. Would the two of you like to come inside? They're about ready."

28

He snuggled in the comfort of her closeness as she patted him. Now and then she sang. The humming of the motor blended with the gentle lapping of water, and sometimes a faraway voice would say, "Little Bits, how ya doin' down there?"

Contentedly Jake stuck his thumb in his mouth and embraced the humming as a friend. But slowly the singing and the humming stopped and he no longer felt the pressure of her body against his side — just an empty space and cool puffs of air.

For one fleeting moment Jake thought about the closeness that was his mother. Then it passed. The only noise was a little trilling bird call that stopped and started sometimes close, now far away.

His eyes blinked once, twice, then opened. Something fluttered on the other side of the room and the whole place smelled of happiness — not like the room where no one smiled and his head hurt all the time.

And who was that guy with the yellow eyes and the big pink mouth? He had stationed himself a few inches away, just sitting and staring as if he wanted to say something. Finally Jake reached out and grabbed the bulbous red nose. The yellow-eyed guy flopped over and squeaked once, then stopped talking. Jake tried answering back. "Shblphatt!"

Now that was a nice sound. He'd try it again. "Plsbb-bbth!" He

191

wouldn't need that other guy to talk to him. He was making lovely sounds all by himself. He could wave his arms, too, and maybe the fluttering things would talk to him. Jake lay very still and focused, pulling his cheeks in and out like a turtle.

Then someone moved in front of the fluttery things — someone with a very dark face and sparkly eyes that held his own like a hug. Jake bubbled his mouth again and the lady picked him up and held him close, talking and moving across the room.

Then one smooth arm lifted near his face and gentled his eyes towards the light. Behind the fluttery things he could see something very tall that rose straight up — it had lots of skinny sticks that were covered with whispery bright specks. That must be where the peaceful smell was coming from, and he pumped his legs up and down so he could get to that tall thing faster.

"Hi there, little Jake. How's my boy today?" Carrie Johnson nuzzled her foster baby and laid him down on the mattress next to a fresh diaper and clean clothes. "Grandpa Will is all ready for you this morning, Sweet One, so let's get you freshened up!"

This honeymoon wasn't at all what he'd planned. First there was that scene at the Elko County Court House. Wasn't Marianna supposed to fall gratefully into his arms when her father showed up? But no, she'd pulled back into her shell again, staying silent and moody even when she'd said "I do" for the Justice of the Peace.

Then, later in the evening, Carver had chosen just the right moment to give her that delicate little silver locket with his picture inside. She'd murmured her thanks and sneezed into a Kleenex.

Carver slumped in his chair and squinted at the window, where the slightly askew motel sign blared on its squatty pole. Then he looked at Marianna, asleep on the bed.

She was always dabbing at her nose with a clump of soggy tissues, and lately her only attempts at conversation had been, "I just don't know, Carver. I just don't know." And on top of that they'd been holed up in one backwater motel after another for nearly five days. Maybe it was time to go home.

Wherever that was. Carver picked a shred of lint off his sweater and folded his arms tightly. Marianna vowed she'd never go back to Cedar Bend. And Carver. . . . Well, he'd rather not stick around home if it meant sharing his father's shame. Furman Adams had been too public, too political. Too . . . crooked. Carver just wanted to hide until everyone had forgotten all about the mayor of Cedar Bend and his ivy league son.

But he and Marianna were running out of money. If they were very careful, there would be just enough cash to get them home at the end of the week. And after that — maybe he'd have to sell the Lexus and get a clunker. Daddy was not likely to mail him allowance checks from jail.

Carver exhaled heavily and flipped open his laptop. He plugged in the modem, then began surfing. Five days on the road and he craved information. Just the look of words lined up neatly on a glowing computer screen or a book or a sheet of white paper energized him. He loved Marianna with all his heart, but sharing information was not exactly her strong suit. Carver Adams could sit and read the phone book and be happy, just as long as he was stuffing himself with new words.

He clicked on the Google icon and poised his tapered brown fingers over the keys. He'd try the Cedar Bend Tribune. Surely news from home would get Marianna's attention. Maybe some high school sports trivia. Her friend Cassie always scored big on the volleyball team.

Cedar Bend Tribune. There! Carver scanned the little folders at the top of the home page. News. Obituaries. Legal notices. Classified. Sports. . . . Sports. Okay, let's try that. Football . . . homecoming against DuPage. Nah. She never liked football. Too brutal.

He grimaced, then glanced over at the bed with its sagging mattress. Marianna hadn't stirred since she'd laid her head on the pillow at eight-fifteen. Her nose was running and her mouth was open. Her whiffly breathing moved her shoulders in a barely perceptible rise and fall, and her black oversized T-shirt contrasted boldly with the faded chenille bedspread.

Carver stared at his little wife for a long time. His eyes stung with unshed tears. *I love you, Baby.*

Absently he bit off some hardened skin near his thumbnail, turned back to the computer and continued scanning through hometown news. He clicked on Legal Notices and scrolled through Unclaimed Funds.

He continued on. Bankruptcy for George Gummers . . . *no one I know* . . . Sheriff's auction . . . 1416 Shirley Drive. *Hmmm — right near the university.* . . .

His fingers froze. Unknown parents . . . abandoned bi-racial infant . . . four to seven weeks old . . . notify Department of Human Services . . . Colchester.

Carver stared at the notice. Colchester. Just fifty miles east of Cedar Bend. Yes, their baby would be almost seven weeks old now, but he was dead, wasn't he?

There was no way he'd share this with Marianna right now. She'd just sog her way through another box of tissues. He shut off the computer and flipped down the lid.

Marianna sneezed again and again into her ever-present moist Kleenex, and each time the bed sank and lifted on her side of the mattress. Another sneeze. She'd wake Carver if she kept this up. Carefully she slid out of the creaking bed. Carver rolled a few inches away from the middle. For most of the night they had curled together like sausages, trapped in the sagging mattress.

Maybe a drink of water. Or a hot washcloth. Mother had always treated Marianna's little illnesses without nonsense. Gargle with salt water. Press a hot washcloth against her face. Chicken soup. Vitamin C. She padded into the bathroom, closed the door and flipped the switch. Her skin was bluish pink in the glaring fluorescent light. Her nose was swollen and purplish and her hair fluttered in limp little wisps about her face.

She put one hand against her flushed cheek, then lifted her T-shirt a few inches and stared long and hard. It had been over six weeks since the surgery, but still there was that angry purple scar near her waistline.

"You're a mess, Mrs. Marianna Adams," she whispered. "What are you going to do about it?"

Funny. A couple of weeks ago Tony had thought about spending the rest of his life here. Now, everywhere he looked, all he could see were things that reminded him of Jake. The empty crib, the nursing bottles stacked neatly in the cupboard, the folded little blankets and pajamas on top of the dresser.

And now that Tony wanted to leave — he couldn't. He'd been "advised" very strongly to stay near Colchester until the investigation was finished. Well, maybe he should be thankful. In a couple of weeks his new home could be prison.

It was late. Almost midnight, and he was still wearing those boots splattered with Jake's blood. He ripped them off in sudden fury and threw them across the room. Then he flung himself onto the bed and molded the feather pillow to his face.

Outside, a fox barked in triumph over her rodent dinner. Then all was still except for the soft honey breezes of late September and the faint lowing of cattle. Gradually Tony's body melted into the sweet heaviness of sleep.

That's when he saw it again — the dirty greasy wheels and the bug-splattered grille. The growling diesel engine and the oily road.

Closer and closer to Angelina, with a hiss of air brakes and the faraway cries of his father.

Only this time, Tony lay dead on the pavement beside his mother.

———————————

"The blood matches."

"You mean the fence?"

"Yeah. There was blood and skin embedded in that oak stick and it matches the baby's. The Number Nine wire was wrapped tight on that stick and fastened with two staples. There's no way he could've used it as a weapon, then wired it back on the fence to cover his story. At least something he told us was right." Investigator Sean McEnroe slapped the folder on the table and rubbed his eyes.

"What else?" FBI Regional Director Manette Currie folded her arms, eyes targeting the men like lasers.

"That burned car checked out." Investigator Roy Burman tilted back on two legs of the cushioned metal chair, arms behind his head. He surveyed the rest of Currie's team. "It belonged to.... Let's see." He bounced the chair back onto four legs and checked his notes. "Beth Lansink. Friend of Tony's. Everyone at the hospital vouches for their friendship. She says she gave Tony her car because he thought he was being followed."

Currie turned to the fire marshal. "What'd you find in the farmhouse? Drugs? Lab stuff?"

"Nothing. Not even one shard of glass other than windows." Gary Cushek looked bewildered by his own statement. "Just evidence of lots of gasoline. Still traces on the burned wood."

"We have good ole Billy Davis Pardiac to thank for that." Roy dug around in his brief case. "Here's his transcript."

Cushek chuckled. "Yeah, good ole Billy the fire bug. There's one guy who won't be out in a long time."

"And there was a tennis shoe. It's in the lockup with the rest of the stuff." Roy checked his notes. "Sheriff Malek found it in the cornfield. Blood on it matches Tony's. Sebastian says the boy's legs and feet were sliced up pretty bad when he found him. Baby had a fresh cut on his arm, too."

He turned back a couple of pages. "All the dates are starting to make sense now. But it sure sounded crazy when I listened to that tape of Billy's a couple of days ago."

"Who's checking out. . . " Currie opened another folder — "Doctor Quaid."

"Billerman. She's over there now, wearing him down. She's working with Ross Schade from Cedar Bend. They're going over all the records in the hospital. They've been talking to the nurses. Says she's got a few bombs ready for us." Roy bit down on his toothpick, trying to keep his lips from curving into a smile.

Doctor Quaid's spacious, airy office was getting very stuffy. The ticking of the little clock on his desk was somehow gaining in volume, like a runaway stop-watch.

Benjamin Quaid tried leaning his elbows on the desk, then pushing his shoulders back against his calfskin office chair — crossing and re-crossing his legs. Anything to keep from sitting still under the steady gaze of Investigators Susan Billerman and Ross Schade. He'd answered the same questions at least four times, and each time to his horror he heard himself putting a different spin on the story he'd so carefully rehearsed with Randy Dupree.

"You say you left the hospital at midnight?"

"Yes."

"That nurse. . . ." Ross flipped a page. "Nurse Dupree says the two of you were in the Operating Room after midnight."

"Oh? Oh, yes, of course. That's right — I went back in the building to ask Randy about another surgery we'd done the day before."

"Which one?"

"I can't remember the name. I'll have to check my computer."

Ross leaned forward. "Mind if we bring Dupree in here with us? We could ask the two of you why there was a crumpled baby wipe behind Autoclave Number One."

Susan Billerman leaned back and tented her hands together. "It had blood on it. Maybe we can check that out too."

29

He couldn't stay here. Not now. Not on this farm where all he ever seemed to do was hurt someone. Tony grabbed jeans and shirts out of the dresser and jammed them into a plastic bag.

They weren't even his clothes, he fumed, just hand-me-downs from Molly's family. Another reminder that he was nothing but a burden. Even the clothes on his back were borrowed.

He'd leave a note for Henry, then maybe thumb a ride back to Cedar Bend. The sooner they were rid of him the better. So what if the Colchester cops came after him. What could be worse than staying in this tomb of a log cabin where his sins rose up to meet him every morning?

He didn't feel bad about taking those ancient boots, though. Henry said no one else ever wore them. The old beat-up leather was discolored where Tony had scrubbed and scraped to get the blood off. Nothing could get out that stain.

He tugged on the boot straps, then stood to have one last look at the sunny room with its little cradle near the window. Abruptly he reached into the closet for Beth's jacket, then remembered he'd hung it in the barn.

Veda must be in the pasture with Henry — he could hear faint shouts punctuated by her sharp yips. No one was in the house, and the front door opened and closed with barely a sound. If only he could shut out the last four weeks of his life that easily!

Tony walked rapidly towards the barn, head down, the bag slung over his shoulder. This wasn't like his first trip around the ranch, when he'd hobbled in sponge-lined boots and looked in awe at the strong gentle woods and the ranch buildings hugging the rocks.

His hand was nearly on the latch of the barn door when he heard a faint singing deep inside the cool interior. Was it a radio? Softly he pulled on one of the double doors and slipped inside. The music was high and sweet, and it was coming from Carrot's old stall.

Tony moved slowly towards the sound. When he came abreast of the first bay, a rustling movement caught his eye. A half-grown heifer stood with head down, one foot hanging limply. She'd tangled her fetlock in a strand of loose barbed wire, and Henry had given her the herbal treatment. Tony felt a tug as he inhaled the familiar deep-forest fragrance. He took two more steps and peered over the partition.

A mop of curly black hair was all he could see, then once again he heard the high piping voice. "Sleep, little one, rest baby dear. Papa and Mama will soon be here."

Nestled in the corner of Carrot's stall, her feet tucked under a horse blanket, Molly sat rocking and singing. She held a tattered rag doll wrapped snugly in a sheet of burlap.

"Don't worry, little Jake. Don't cry. Tony didn't mean to hurt you." She stroked the faded gray face. "It was a accil-dent." She hummed again, holding the baby inside the curve of her neck as she swayed back and forth.

Tony's throat caught in a sob. Molly turned at the sound, then struggled to her feet. "Tony! Tony! Oh, Uncle Tony! Jake wants you!" She held out the little bundle, her face alight with joy. "Look. He saw you and stopped crying!"

Tony reached for the rag doll and it seemed the most natural thing in the world to hold it close. Another cry rose in his throat and suddenly it was as if a great weight was pushing him down to the barn floor. He crumpled against the stable wall and began sobbing in great heaves.

"Tony, oh Tony. Don't cry. Don't cry." Molly reached for his arm. "It'll be okay." She patted her hand along his sleeve in little fluttery motions, then sat quietly leaning against his shoulder.

When Tony's cries had melted to a whisper she turned her face up to his.

"God told me a secret last night." She lowered her eyes almost shyly. "Jake's gonna go home, Tony. He's gonna get to go home."

This was the ninth call she'd had about the baby, and Christa was just about ready to throw the phone across the room. She didn't know what all those people might want with a foundling kid but it was clear they couldn't even begin to prove a relationship to little Baby August. Now here was this young girl on the phone — sounded about fifteen — who said she thought Jake was hers.

Christa sighed and took another swig of her diet pop. *Okay, okay. Act your age, Christa. Make the appointment with this kid. That's what you're here for.* "Yes. Yes. Mm-hm."

She straightened suddenly, dropped her pen. "Uh, yes, sure. Just, um." She scrolled down her Palm Pilot. "If you can get here by five-fifteen I can see you and your . . . um . . . husband . . . today. Yes, Honey. Just come into the main office. It's Department of Human Services at three-twenty Broadway. And ask for me. I'm Christa Jamison."

Randy Dupree knocked softly. Benjamin Quaid unfolded his long legs from the office chair and shuffled, bent like an old man, towards the paneled door. He opened it and touched Randy lightly on the shoulder, guiding him towards the couch before returning to his seat behind the desk. The two conspirators faced each other across the room.

Benjamin sat so silently and for so long that Randy began to sweat.

Finally the doctor's lips moved. His words came in a quiet monotone. "I'm going to come clean about the surgery."

Randy swallowed once, opened his mouth, then changed his mind and closed it.

"I don't think there's anything I can say that would let you know how sorry I am."

Randy waited. He wouldn't talk just yet. Let the good doctor do the sweating this time.

"I will do everything I can to convince the authorities that this was not your idea." Quaid cleared his throat. "That you . . . performed under duress."

Randy kept his voice flat. "You'll tell the police, you mean."

"Obviously. That's the first step. But it's the hospital board I'm most concerned about. You see," Quaid got up and turned sideways to the window, a strange smile working its way across his face. "They'll strip me down, Randy. No more hospital privileges. And, sooner or later, no more license."

Randy exhaled slowly, closed his eyes and leaned back. His arms went limp.

"I expect they'll do the same to you." A pause. "You have been a professional in every sense of the word. But no more. No more." He shuddered. "I am so very, very sorry."

"Why did you do it, Ben?"

Dr. Quaid turned his head sharply at the sudden familiar use of his nickname. Then he paused, rubbed one hand slowly across the other, examining his long slender fingers first on one side, then the other. "Have you ever met Helene Morrow?"

"I've seen her. That's all."

"If you do not know her, there is no way I can explain to you the kind of power she held over me." Benjamin straightened. "I say

202

'held over me.' She no longer has me in her grip, Randy. I have come to terms with who I am. And with who my God is. I no longer fear her." His eyes glistened and his chin lifted slightly. "You called me Ben just now."

Randy leaned forward, glaring at Quaid. "Yes. . . . Yes, I did." He straightened, folded his arms. "But for this question I will call you by your official title."

He stared long and hard at his former boss. "Tell me, Doctor Quaid, why you needed me to finish the job. Why didn't you just perform a simple Dilation and Extraction?" He grimaced. "That would have been safer . . . at least for one of your patients." Quaid looked up sharply as Randy finished. "Then you could have done everything yourself. Nice and neat."

Ben stiffened. He stepped closer to the window, then slowly turned to face Randy. "I . . . didn't want. . . ." His voice caught, then with supreme effort he worked his face into a ghastly smile. "You wouldn't do it either, you know, if you could help it." Still with the same frozen expression, Ben focused on a high corner of the room and stood clenching and unclenching his hands.

He straightened suddenly, fixed Randy's eyes with his. "Have you ever witnessed a Dilation and Extraction?"

"No. The D and X was . . . voluntary at my school."

"Believe me, you would never volunteer for this." Ben slid open his desk drawer and pulled out a pair of long scissors. He held them up and turned them several ways to the light. "Would you like to try it? Here. Hold this like so."

He walked slowly towards the sofa and slid the cold instrument into Randy's hand, pressing the nurse's fingers tightly around the closed handles. "These are just crude scissors for cutting paper. "Surgical scissors are finely honed, as you know. Very strong. Very sharp. Very exact."

Randy began to sweat again.

Dr. Quaid was leaning over, covering the scissors and Randy's hands with both of his. He began to squeeze — tighter and tighter until Randy cried out.

Ben whispered to Randy while he slowly released his grip. "Would you ever want to put these scissors into the back of a baby's head?"

Suddenly Ben straightened and stumbled back to his chair. Both sat still and spent. After a moment Randy wiped his forehead on a sleeve.

Ben was the first to speak. "The answer to the other part of your question is 'no.' In my opinion a cesarean is not more dangerous than a D & X. Not when it's done right."

He began to chuckle — low and rasping. "But my professional opinion won't matter any more. We're just two ordinary men now, Randy. Men with feet of clay. Nobody will think of our titles anymore. No more 'Chief of Obstetrics Doctor Quaid' for me.

"No more 'Registered Nurse Randy Dupree' for you.

"All of our power is draining away. . . . Perhaps that is the first step towards healing. For both of us."

The old plank floors at Town and Country Outfitters dipped and creaked.

In this aisle, a pair of stiff leather boots.

Up the center — a Western navy blue shirt with pearled buttons. Now back in the corner for straight-leg jeans and adobe-calf-skin belt.

"Would you like to top it off with a Stetson?" Henry was trying very hard to keep his mouth straight.

"I'm about as duded up as I'd like to be, thanks." Tony surveyed himself in the pitted mirror. His curly hair was slicked back, still damp at the edges from the quick shower this morning. Henry had told him to hurry and grab his stuff and jump in the Silverado. There was a friend who wanted to see him.

"Good. Let's get going."

Carrie Johnson was not going to disturb this hallowed moment, this blending of joy and sorrow. She sat far back in the corner of the little government room, fanning herself with a handkerchief. Department of Human Services Investigator Christa Jamison stood by the door, arms crossed, eyes alert — blocking the cheerless hallway. Henry, leaning against the wall, tried his best to recede into the woodwork.

Near the window Tony stood with the baby, his strong profile sharp against the sheen of rising day. Jake had settled his hand on Tony's finger, frowning in concentration, pursing his lips and working his mouth.

They stayed for nearly ten minutes this way, taking each other's measure. Then the baby's eyelids grew heavy with sleep, and Tony gently released the tiny hand and gave his son back into the arms of the DHS.

30

"Just turn your head. Don't look. It'll go faster that way. Okay, relax your fist and keep your arm on the table." Lab technician Mindy Walters deftly inserted the needle into Marianna's right arm. Dark red blood flowed in a steady stream, filling the sample vial.

"Got it! You did great. Now, hold this piece of cotton against your arm. I'll just wrap it with gauze. That's it. Keep it there for about an hour."

Mrs. Marianna Adams stayed frozen to her chair.

"It's okay, Sugar. We're all done now. You can get up. Ooops. Just a minute. I keep dropping stuff." Mindy retrieved her pencil. "It's been one crazy week in here, know what I mean? We were about ready to close up shop. You're lucky you both came when you did."

She popped her gum. "Oh, and don't worry. The lab results go straight to the Department. There's a whole new technique for those DNA tests now, so we might even get them back on Tuesday. They'll be sure to contact you, probably Wednesday."

Mindy flipped out her marking pen, labeled the two vials and put them in a small rack on her desk.

Carver and Marianna walked out the door of the century-old building and stood uncertainly in the cool twilight.

Marianna looked imploringly into her husband's face. "It's Friday. We have to wait four whole days."

She took his hand and shivered in the night air. "Carver." She
snuggled next to him. "I'd really like to go back to Cedar Bend and
see Cassie."

Carver frowned. "Yes. Well, I guess we do need some stuff at the
mall. Let's do that, and then you can see her." He was rewarded with
one of her sudden smiles. "Wait. Let's find a motel first. I'll go with
you to the mall, drop you at Cassie's, then check the Internet. You
can just call me when you're ready."

A covert look at his watch. Four nights. Maybe more. He made a
quick calculation. So far the money was holding out. . . .

"I guess a few days won't hurt." Carver opened the door to
their newest purchase — a rusted hatchback. He was fascinated, as
always, with the way his wife melted into the car in one graceful
ballet motion.

———

Beth Lansink fidgeted. Nervously she twined Randy Dupree's fingers with her own. On the circular bench attached to the tree trunk,
they were half hidden under the spreading maple.

"I don't get it. What could be worse than what you've been going
through the last few weeks? I'm sick and tired of secrets."

Randy pulled his hand away, resting his elbows on his knees.

Beth studied him for a long time. Then she let out a disgusted
sigh. "Look at you! There's not a free bone in your body. Let it go,
Randy. Just tell them the truth. Tell them everything."

She put both hands on his face and turned it towards her. "I'll
stand by you."

Randy leaned back, took her hand again. They sat quietly
watching the parade of mall shoppers. "You've never let me down,
Beth. I . . . don't know anyone I can trust like that."

"Yeah." Her grin was open and free. She punched his shoulder.
Hard.

"Ow! So much for trust. You could break my arm, you know."

It was Friday — people-watching night at the newly renovated Mall of the Dome. The quadrangle was filling rapidly with high school kids and dreamy-eyed couples. In front of Bingley's Sporting Goods a tall young man put his arm around the girl next to him. She leaned towards him, then withdrew.

Beth and Randy could not decide whether she was slim or stout. The only thing they could see was that she was short. From her neck to her knees she was nearly swallowed in a voluminous flannel shirt. Perhaps it belonged to the nervous young man beside her, so properly dressed in dockers and button-down oxford.

"I know who that is." Randy leaned forward. "I . . . know . . . who . . . that . . . girl . . . is." He put his head into his hands, then savagely scrubbed his fingers through his wiry hair. After a long moment he looked up and took a deep breath. He stood and kissed Beth lightly on the top of her head.

"Wait for me."

31

"**B**aby . . . Baby. Look. We'll just have to be patient." Carver held Marianna in a tight embrace, willing her to stop crying, stop shuddering. She had been weeping most of the night, and twice he'd stopped her from grabbing the keys and bolting for the car.

"Sh-h-h. Sh-h-h. No one else is going to take him, Marianna."

He smoothed his hands along her shoulders, cradling her head against his chest. "Tuesday will come soon, and then it will all work out. You'll see. We've done the DNA tests. There's nothing else we can do."

"But who's taking care of him? He's lonely. Maybe he's still hurt. What if. . . ."

"Just . . . just sit down a minute, okay? Look. From what Randy says, Tony's a good guy. He rescued our baby, risked his life. He wouldn't let anything happen. . . ."

"But he did. He *did* let something happen to him!" Marianna shuddered again, remembering with horror the story she'd heard from Randy Dupree last night. "Oh Carver, you've got to do something! We can't just sit around here!"

Wearily she took in the orange drapes, the shiny green bedspread and the stained carpet.

"Okay, listen." Carver released Marianna and walked over to the window. "I've got an idea. Remember Jed Carlucci? He graduated with me — left school before I started my Masters."

Marianna nodded, wiping her nose. "Well, I think he's working for Department of Human Services right here in Red Hawk County." Carver stepped to the side table and picked up a phone book. "I'll call him. He should know something about how this stuff works. These government programs are probably the same all over the state."

Marianna blew her nose. She wasn't saying anything. But at least she had stopped crying.

"There's a lot I don't know." Jed crumpled his Burger King wrapper and took a sip of iced tea, then opened a hefty three-ring notebook. "But at least I can give you some guidelines. Oh, Man! Sometimes it's pretty confusing. There's policy on top of programs, then there's protocol to make sure you get the policy right."

Marianna nodded numbly.

"Okay. Here's the place to start. Your baby had a . . . well, a surprising . . . beginning, to say the least." Marianna studied the lettuce in her salad. "Look, I didn't mean. . . ." She nodded, gave a brief tight smile.

"Okay. Anyway, here's what I know. For DHS purposes, your baby's status probably got started in the middle of what we usually call a nine-step process. Now he's being treated as a 'child of unknown origin.' The first place DHS will start is to try to find the parents."

Carver leaned forward, frowning in concentration.

"I did some checking into this. Made a couple of calls. It's kind of complicated because at the same time, there's an ongoing investigation involving Tony Kowalski. The county attorney's got his hands in it, so the whole process is going to move forward pretty fast. At least for now." Marianna glanced up sharply. "And, at the same time, DHS will investigate . . . um . . . things . . . and see whether they need to keep the baby in foster care."

Both Marianna and Carver remained motionless. Jed flipped a page and continued. "Your baby's in foster care because of the injury, and because. . . ."

Marianna studied Jed with narrowed eyes.

". . . because they may have found evidence of an earlier injury. And that could mean . . . at least suggest . . . regular abuse."

Marianna covered her face and moaned. Her shoulders tightened. Across the aisle a construction worker had stopped chewing, more interested in the drama unfolding at the next table than in his Monday lunch.

Jed groped for some good news. "Hey. You've got your DNA tests started. Hopefully this week sometime they'll know you're the parents." Marianna folded two delicate hands under her chin.

Well, Jed thought. Might as well plunge ahead with the not so good news and get it over with. "It, um, could be just a tad longer, though. I've only been in DHS six months but I already know that not everything . . . well . . . let's just say it doesn't always go the way you want it to."

Marianna, two tissues pressed against her nose, rose abruptly and headed for the rest room.

"Hey, I'm sorry, man."

"It's a mess, Jed. Marianna keeps blaming herself." Carver fixed his eyes on the window, absently studying the cars coming into the parking lot. "She's on a real roller coaster ride. Full of hope one minute, and just plain guilty the next."

There was a long pause. Carver's mouth had begun to work strangely, and he tightened his arms across his chest. Suddenly he whipped his head around and pounded a fist into his palm. "Her mother and the doctor both lied to her. That's why she went through with this . . . this. . . ."

Jed leaned back in his chair. He'd never been really close to the cool, collected Carver, and the last thing he expected from him was raw emotion. He shuffled some papers, checked his watch and cleared his throat. "I . . . um, well. Tell you what. When Marianna comes back I'll just hit the high points real fast and let the two of you have some time to yourselves, and then you can call me if you've got any more questions." He turned his head towards the aisle and stared pointedly at the construction worker, who took the hint and stalked off with his tray.

Marianna came back to the table, her hair dampened in little clusters around her face. "I . . . I'm okay now."

"Look," Jed began. "I know this hasn't been easy for you. But here's what you've got to know. Maybe this will help if the thing starts to drag out."

Carver looked anxiously at Marianna, expecting her eyes to start watering again, but she sat straight, her shoulders rigid.

"DHS has a juggling act. They've got to find the parents at the same time they're trying to figure out whether Tony is a child abuser — or, if he's cleared of all suspicion, whether he's a legitimate guardian." Another sip of iced tea. Marianna sat poised with a fresh tissue. "Meanwhile, Jake will stay in foster care."

Carver jotted some notes, while Marianna sat still as a stone. "Usually with child abuse, DHS puts a team together, and tries counseling and other stuff to get the child back to his parents. But, since they don't know who the parents are. . . ."

Jed held up a hand when he saw a glint of fire in Marianna's eyes. "Since they don't know, they go on the presumption that he doesn't have any. Or at least they put him in foster care until the parents or other relatives can be found."

Nervously, Jed glanced at Marianna, then continued. He'd sure like to finish this conversation. The little Burger King table was so electric it could generate its own storm cover.

"Your baby already has his own Guardian ad Litem appointed by Juvenile Court." He could see trouble in their faces again, and held up one hand. "Ad Litem just means 'for the suit.' They want a third party to represent the child and protect his interests."

Jed flipped over a few pages, showed them a drawing of stairsteps. There were nine steps, each labeled with a Child In Need of Assistance procedure.

"Now on this top step — Assessment/Intake — that's where they'd start if they got a complaint against the parents or guardian about some kind of child abuse. But we're well beyond this now."

Jed pointed to the fourth step, Removal. "That's where the baby was taken away from Tony. So, right now, you'd be at least on step five — Adjudication."

"Ad-ju-what?" Marianna looked at Jed, her forehead creased in a frown.

Carver put a hand on her shoulder. "Adjudication. It's Latin. It means to judge the truth of something by looking at all sides."

Marianna shrugged away from his hand. "I didn't ask *you!*" she mumbled. "I asked *him.*" Carver folded his hands in his lap and looked away. Jed busied himself with his pencil.

"Or, you could be at the sixth step — Disposition — which is a kind of tentative agreement about where the baby will finally wind up." He moved quickly to the next step — Review. "Now here's where they just see if all the steps are making sense and moving along in the right direction."

He tapped his pencil on Step Nine. "But here's the payoff. Here's where you want to be — *Permanency.*"

32

"She told you Tuesday?" Christa checked her Palm Pilot. "That's not very realistic. Well, yes, but . . . I'm sure she meant that Tuesday would be the soonest. Yes. Mm-hm. I know it's Wednesday. Yes, I understand. We're doing everything we can here. Yes. Yes, I know you are. Would you want to try back in a couple of. . . . *Hello?*"

There were only fifteen minutes left until her meeting with Judge Bickle. Well, Christa could spare two minutes, anything to ward off the hysteria she'd heard on the phone just now.

She dialed the clinic. "It's Christa at DHS. You did a blood test for Marianna and Carver Adams on Friday. Yes, and one for Baby August." She spelled the names. "They're not back yet? Could you please check your computer files, or call Bennington Lab — see what stage those reports are in right now?"

Christa started working on the other half of her cherry Pop Tart, brushing the crumbs into a napkin. "Yes, okay. It's Mar-i-an-na Ad-ams. Yes, and Car-ver Ad-ams. Uh huh. You got the spelling? Well okay. Sure, I'll wait."

She'd just jammed the end of the pastry into her mouth when the voice crackled over the phone again. She sat frozen, then suddenly slapped the portable phone hard into her other hand. "You. Don't. Have. Any. Record. Of. . . ."

There was a long pause, and not just because she was gagging on Pop Tart flakes.

"Look, you're making an appointment for that Adams couple right now. No, I don't care how busy you are. They were in your shop Friday. They did everything they were supposed to do, and this is one time I'm not going to make my clients wait just because something was lost. This afternoon, three-fifteen, then."

She tapped the off button and tossed the phone onto the desk, where it slid across a dab of cherry jelly before coming to rest against her brief case.

———————————

Shoot. He didn't know where to go and what to do when he got there. Should he kneel or stand. Should he fold his hands. Bow his head? *Okay, okay, just do it, man.* Tony stumbled across the uneven pasture and headed for the walnut tree. He settled onto the ground with his back against the gnarled trunk, tossing a smooth white stone from hand to hand.

The air was crisp and cool, and a steady wind rustled through the heavy grasses, flipping their tops like flags. A few yards behind the fence a dozen cows grazed methodically, their long raspy tongues raking into fresh pasture.

"It's just you and me, God." Tony dropped the stone and leaned back, closed his eyes. "I guess maybe I'm like David. At least that part about messing up. Big time."

He opened his eyes, watched a calf trotting to the next clump of succulent grass. "But I don't really know how to be a man after . . . you know . . . your own heart." He hesitated. "If that means being sorry, then I qualify big time, because I'm . . . I'm sorry I. . . ." His voice trailed off and his eyes began to sting.

"Jake needs you too, even more than I do." He brushed his sleeve across his face. "And whatever that grace is — you know, the kind from Jesus that Henry talked about, I could use a big dose of that. The blotting out kind, I mean." He shrugged his shoulders, then let them grow limp. His hands slowly rested on the ground, palms facing the sky.

After awhile he looked up, squinting briefly at the blood-red sun. He watched as one brilliant white cloud changed shape rapidly, pushed along by the wind.

FBI regional director Manette Currie liked a bit of drama. In the conference room of the county attorney's suite she had set out pitchers of water, glasses, napkins and fresh copies of the latest interagency report on Antonio Kowalski and Baby August. She buttoned her navy blazer, then sat in the power seat at the head of the table. There would be high drama today when the investigation team saw her wrap-up. She checked her watch and waited.

County Attorney Barry Peterman came in first, gave Manette a measured glance and a nod, then sat at the other end of the table and poured himself a glass of ice water. He looked around at the crisp white reports. This could be a power play if he'd let it. No. He wouldn't go there.

By the time Christa Jamison had parked herself in the seat nearest the door, all the chairs next to the stapled reports were filled except one.

Manette tented her hands, her manicured fingertips lightly brushing her lips. She surveyed the table, ticking off the names of the investigators in her head. Roy Burman, Susan Billerman and Sean McEnroe from Colchester Police, Ross Schade of the Cedar Bend Police Department, Christa Jamison of DHS, and County Attorney Barry Peterman.

She scanned quickly for the Regional Fire Marshal: "Where's Cushek?"

"Fire at Liberty. He'll be late if he gets here at all."

"Well, then, let's get started."

Benjamin Quaid was not surprised when Shannon Memorial Chief of Staff Wendell Graber stopped him near the OR and laid a kindly hand on his shoulder, beaming his sad, grandfatherly smile. "You free for lunch tomorrow?" It wasn't an invitation. It was a directive.

Ben turned tired eyes towards his mentor of twenty plus years, warmed by the sorrow and compassion in the lined face. "Depends. Are you buying?" He'd keep it light, draw it out. He could wait.

"For you, Ben, always. Let's meet at the Pecan Tower. One o'clock? Avoid the crowds." Wendell's grip tightened, staking his claim.

"I'll be there."

Grace did not let go of his arm until she'd seated him securely next to Henry. Tony remembered later that it was not so much the soft touch of his attorney's hand or the sense of quiet that he felt in her office that day, but a total disconnect from reality as she walked the final seven steps around the burnished walnut desk, seating herself across from them.

Tony watched with fascination as she laid out a file, smoothed a couple of papers, adjusted her pen, then folded her hands.

Her first words were like body blows.

"I don't believe in drawing things out. What I have to tell you is very difficult." She pressed her hands tightly together, as if to hold them in check. Tony noticed the air space between her wedding ring and her finger. The knuckles from her other hand were pushing it up from underneath as her grip tightened.

"A man and a woman have made a claim of parenthood. Their DNA tests match Jake's." She paused, holding Tony's eyes with hers, studying his resolve. His expression had not changed.

Henry, his massive frame tense and still, was watchful.

"But I'll get back to that." She turned over the folder, opened another one. "The good news, Tony, is that you will not be charged. With anything. No abuse, no child stealing, no negligence. Nothing. They've corroborated every word of your testimony."

Tony still had not moved. Henry suddenly remembered the shell-shocked ball-turret gunner he'd seen in the hospital ward when he was a child — the same staring eyes, the slack mouth, the limp, motionless body.

Grace continued cautiously. "DHS will make their recommendations to the Juvenile Court judge, and there will be at least one hearing."

Henry came to the rescue. "A hearing. So — this is not an open and shut case? Is there any chance. . . ."

"There is always an outside chance."

She flipped through papers from file to file, more to keep her hands busy than to reveal new information. Grace had memorized each heartbreaking detail by heart. "It's possible that they could find these parents totally irresponsible, or decide they acted negligently by abandoning their baby."

"Then," Tony started, barely above a whisper, "I might have a chance?" There was that weight of silence again. His ears sharpened to the buzz of a fly on the window sill, the faint hum of fluorescent lights.

"In my experience. . . . " She coughed once, started again. "In my experience, no. There is practically no chance at all. Nearly always, unless the parents have shown a pattern of abuse, they will have first priority." She leaned back, folded her arms. "We could fight this." Tony raised his head. "But I would not recommend it."

Mr. and Mrs. Adams had a right to a lawyer. They had a right to request financial assistance to pay for that lawyer. They had a right to speak out. They had a right to a hearing. Yes. And even a right to see their baby. For one hour. Tomorrow. With the DHS watching every step.

And tomorrow morning was already here. Two-fifteen on the tiny illuminated digital clock by her bedside. Seven more hours until the appointment.

Marianna reviewed it once more in her mind. They should get there early. Dress conservatively. Speak when spoken to. Answer calmly and politely.

But they had not told her what it would be like to hold her Little Bits for the first time. Over and over she had walked through the scene — and over and over she had imagined herself grabbing the baby and running for the car, where she and Carver would escape this nightmare of Ad-ju-di-cation and Guardian ad Li-TUM!! They would be possessed of super-human strength, this reunited family in their little rusted hatchback, escaping a thousand police cars and heading for Canada where they would live happily ever after.

Marianna clutched her damp Kleenex and stifled a sob. Then she willed herself to relax. She would need some sleep to look fresh in the morning. No sense scaring her baby half to death.

On the other side of the bed Carver studied the blinking lights just visible through a chink in the drapes. The traffic light at First Street had been flashing red for three hours. A little while ago he had counted the blinks to a hundred and fifty.

Then he had begun worrying about his role in the upcoming drama. Until now all this business about having a baby was just story-book. On paper. It was a role he had been able to savor at his own pace. Today, in a few short hours, he would be a real father. He would hold his baby, with Marianna leaning her lovely head on his arm. He'd practiced the walk, the calm assurance, the quiet nod to the government representatives. He would be in charge.

"Marianna?" She shifted. Turned towards him. He enfolded her in his arms and closed his eyes. They did not waken until the little clock reminded them of the most important day of their lives.

33

His head was burning. He couldn't eat because he couldn't breathe. And where was his sweet milk? What had happened to the good stuff? Jake whipped his mouth away from the bottle, spluttering and howling.

"Listen, Will. I don't care what the doctor says. We're not giving him any more of that canned junk. You run over to Henry's and get some fresh milk."

Carrie straightened to her full five feet and glowered at her husband. "Of course Henry knows we've got the baby! He's got two ears and two eyes! Now you just get over there. Milk that goat yourself if you have to!"

She looked at the fretful baby in her arms. "Mercy! How will it be to bring this child all hot and fussy to meet his mama for the first time." She smoothed back the blanket, cradled Jake against her shoulder and rocked gently from one foot to another. Slowly the crying stopped.

Jake hiccuped and moaned softly, then his body grew limp under Carrie's steady hand, and he drifted into an uneasy sleep.

Henry walked into the entryway and took off his boots, then let out one staccato command: "TONY! Sheilah needs some attention.

You and Molly go fix her up."

Tony's mouth opened, ready for questions, but before he could say anything Henry loaded his arms with bandages, ointments and scissors.

"Molly's home from school today. She'll know what to do."

Henry waved vaguely and headed for the office, his shoulders bent under the weight of fatigue. Tony looked down at his oddly-assorted bundle. No sense talking to Henry when he got like that. Just head for the barn and take care of that little goat.

This had been a weird day from the first moment gray light had filtered into Tony's room. He'd decided, once again, to stay at Henry's, but each new day seemed disconnected from the one before it.

Somehow Grace Longstreet had learned about the DHS visit scheduled for later this morning, and that was the first thing he'd thought about at daybreak. Today the "real" mother and father would go and stake their claim on Jake, and here he would be — out of sight, out of mind. Yet for some reason all of the bitterness and despair seemed to have floated away while he slept.

Happy? He could not call it that. Not even a little bit. He was . . . resting. Resting deep inside himself, in a place he'd never been able to reach before. Yes. That was it, he thought, struggling to balance the jumble of instruments and bandages clutched to his chest.

Inside the vast cool barn Molly was already practicing her own brand of medicine with soft caresses and a whispered lullaby. In the second stall she stood directly in front of Sheilah, her small hands gently massaging the stiff ears.

The little goat leaned the full weight of her neck and head against Molly's chest, eyes closed in dreamy ecstasy, her tail wagging like a dog's. On her neck a jagged wound glistened, seeping red against coarse black hair.

Molly giggled a greeting, then she was all business. "Put that on the table behind you." She pushed gently on the goat's rump and squeezed out of the stall.

"Let's go and clean our hands." She turned towards the wash room, and Tony could hear splashing and rinsing, then a soft scrubbing with a towel. He rolled up his sleeves. Time to get clean, dig into the work.

Molly's eyes glittered with mischief and purpose. "Now you put some of that Calendula on that little soft rag. Yeah . . . that one. And I'll wash her cut." She gestured with stiff, quick movements. "You'd better stand back."

Once more she opened the gate and stepped into the stall. The little goat, her legs splayed, opened sleepy eyes a few inches, then closed them again, resting in the attention.

At the first touch, Sheilah's head lifted dreamily, then settled again, as Molly wiped her cut with the cool Calendula gel, her strokes deft and sure.

"Now, Tony. Hand me those little scissors." Again the quick movement of the little hands as she clipped hair around the cut, careful not to touch open flesh.

Then, once more with the Calendula and a second order to Tony: "Now the long cloth." She looked up, her eyes pleading. "Would you help me?" Tony moved cautiously into the stall, bandage in hand.

Molly kept her voice low. "Here. You hold it on the top of her neck and I'll loop it under. Then you bring it up again. Twice." Quietly they worked side by side, against a background of the goat's steady breathing and a flutter of pigeons in the loft.

"Now the pin." Tony stepped out of the stall again, found the industrial-sized safety pin, and handed it to Molly.

"No, you pin it. Up there on top of her neck."

Oh boy, all I need now is to jab this old goat. With shaking hands Tony fastened the heavy pin. Sheilah lifted her bored oval face, then settled back into her favorite pastime — sleep. Molly and Tony stepped quietly out of the stall, latched it, then stood and looked at each other.

Molly cocked her head to one side, her hands clasped in front of her. A shy smile played around her lips, then widened to a grin.

"You can do more than you think you can, Tony."

He'd heard that before. They were Henry's words.

Slowing after their interstate exit, Carver and Marianna drove down the long hill towards Main Street, then passed the ancient courthouse with its weathered stone steps and stout wooden door. Three stories tall, it sported curly filigrees at the top, much like a stale gingerbread house. Tacked onto the back of the building, the Dover County Sheriff's Department had made a faint stab at the twentieth century with its low sloping roof and glass-brick windows.

Hugging Seventh Street two blocks north, an architectural marvel crouched near the sidewalk. It was an amalgam of several portly buildings of varying history, including a ninety-year-old bank. And in the likely event that someone should mistake this jumble of edifices for anything else, over the main door a modest brass sign announced: "Department of Human Services."

Carver turned off the motor and kept his hand briefly on the key. This was it. This really was it. But what was "it"? He didn't know. He'd just keep walking through this event as if he knew what he was doing. Get out of the car. Open the door for Marianna. Walk down the cracked, uneven sidewalk five steps, open the stiff glass and aluminum door.

Marianna had begun shivering the moment they'd left their room an hour earlier. Swathed in one of Carver's flannel shirts, she'd hugged her arms tightly for the entire trip. The new husband and wife, acutely aware that they were father and mother, did not speak as they walked endlessly down first one hall, then another, following the little arrowed signs to the second-floor conference room.

Funny how she hadn't noticed before, Marianna thought, that Carver's long stride never seemed to fit her short steps. She tried matching his gait, then switched to taking two steps for each one of his. That didn't work either, and the untried parents filled the hallway with the sound of four feet all searching for order.

Christa Jamison met them on the second landing.

"Good morning, Carver and Marianna."

She came alongside and laid a motherly hand on the girl's shoulder, pointing with the other. "Mrs. Johnson's in that room right down there. She and her husband have been taking care of the baby." (Better not say *your* baby yet!) "She and I will stay with you for the visit."

From the room there issued a faint wailing. Suddenly Marianna stopped. She shook her head slowly from side to side, nostrils flaring. Her eyes widened in horror. "I can't. I can't go in there."

"What?" Carver had walked a few steps past her, then realized she wasn't keeping pace. "Baby, what's the matter! What is it?"

Marianna tried to un-wad her soggy Kleenex. "He . . . he hates me." She dabbed at her eyes. "He knows I'm coming." She covered her face with shaking hands, then turned abruptly and buried her head against Carver's sleeve, her muted sobs drifting down the hallway.

Marianna and Carver could hear the wailing more clearly now. It had changed to angry blasts.

"Excuse me. Just a minute." Christa walked quickly into the room, closed the door. There was a muffled conversation, a few hiccups, then a spluttering sucking sound.

The door opened again and the baby's foster mother emerged, a sad smile lighting her warm brown face. Carrie Johnson walked directly to Marianna and gently folded the young mother into her plump arms.

"Sh-h-h. . . . Sh-h-h. Hush now, Sweet One. Hush. You just let Mother Carrie worry about that baby. He's hungry, that's all. Just woke up yelling for his breakfast. Miz Jamison has him now, and he's workin' mighty hard on that milk!"

Marianna clung tightly to Carrie, and slowly her sobbing shuddered to a stop. Behind them the door opened, and Marianna caught a glimpse of her Little Bits, his delicate hands clutched tightly to a bottle of fresh goat milk, his mouth working with all its strength to pull the entire contents into his body in one gulp.

Marianna froze. She wanted to lift her arms, take her baby in both hands — take her away from Christa. But she could not move.

Carrie motioned to Carver and Marianna with her chin while she gathered Jake in her arms. "You two sit over there. Let us come to you."

Carrie stood holding the baby for a few moments, laughing and talking to Jake as she let him finish his dinner. "There's someone here to see you. Now you be a good boy and say *hello*." She tucked the faded blanket more tightly around the little feet, planted a soft kiss on his head, then laid him gently on Marianna's lap.

Jake, rested from his nap and restored through Sheilah's good milk, lay very still. He lifted one arm outside the blanket, and for a moment it looked very much as if he were waving. He pushed his tiny fist into his cheek and the left side of his mouth curled into a lopsided smile.

Then he smacked his lips and stared at the two faces. One was scowling and one was all screwed up in pain. But nobody was saying anything. Why not!? People usually talked to him.

Maybe he should talk first. "Shlbt!" They were getting interested now. No more frowns. This was more like it. He'd try it again.

"Blshppshth!" Ooops. Jake's effort was starting something on the other end that he'd probably better finish.

Now the room was an explosion of mixed utterances, and joining in the loudest were Carver and Marianna, their fears released to laughter.

34

Carver Adams squirmed in his chair. He didn't want to look at the slim blond woman in the power suit, focusing instead on the court reporter's short fingers hovering over the keys. This was the second day of the Permanency Hearing and nothing seemed to be going right. He and Marianna so far had managed to look like candidates for World's Worst Parents.

"Would you repeat the question please?"

"What are your plans for employment?" Guardian ad Litem Jodene Taylor smiled tightly, her silver pen balanced gracefully between two polished fingernails. "That's not a hard question, is it?"

Carver tried to focus on something else besides Jodene Taylor. His eyes darted around the newly remodeled Courtroom Two — a tiny space filled with state of the art Scandinavian furniture, and just enough chairs for attorneys, witnesses and one row of spectators. For a moment he focused on a little girl who sat clutching the arm of a frowning young man with dark, curly hair.

The east wall was banked with tall glass windows tightly held in place by aluminum frames. There was no provision for opening them to the fresh outdoors.

The skinny clock hand on the back wall jiggled slightly as it worked its way upwards towards Twelve. Reluctantly Carver moved his gaze back to Jodene, gripping his hands tightly. "I . . . was hoping to finish my Masters in Library Science. Then . . . then I would try to find a job."

Jodene let her pen drop. She scooted her chair back a few inches, tenting her hands in front of her face. "And what will you live on in the meantime?"

"Well, I . . . I mean we . . . have three thousand dollars in the bank from the sale of our Lexus." He stopped, thinking through this trap. What exactly did she want to hear? "I have an application at McDonald's. At least for now."

"When do you . . . *hope* . . . to finish your masters?"

"Probably next May."

"Probably. Mm-hm. Let's see." She flipped through her note pad. "Three thousand dollars in the bank. No home address. An application at McDonald's for minimum wage. Doing your Masters work in between. Your wife still a junior in high school."

Jodene's smile was grim. "Mr. Adams, your father and Marianna's mother are both both being held on several charges. Their assets are legally frozen."

There was a terrible pause. "Maybe. Probably. Hopefully. That does not sound very hopeful to me. Just how do you plan to support a family with this plan?"

"By . . . by working hard."

The entire courtroom seemed to be sucked into a vacuum of silence. There was no response from Jodene Taylor. Just a vague smile as she scribbled on her note pad.

"That is sufficient for this line of questioning, Ms. Taylor."

Jodene flipped all the pages down on her curled notepad. "No further questions, your Honor."

Juvenile Judge Margaret Bickle tilted her chin towards Carver. "You may step down, Mr. Adams."

Carver shifted, preparing to rise, when he caught the eye of his attorney, Sam Bella, who was motioning first to the witness chair and then to Judge Bickle.

The judge scanned her list. "We have time for one more. Mr. Bella, you may proceed." A whispered groan floated through the room as several attorneys glanced at the clock: Eleven fifty-one.

Christa Jamison leaned forward, shuffled a few papers and brushed a strand of hair away from her face. She laid a hand on Sam's shoulder and mouthed, "Wait."

Christa fumbled for a pen that would actually work.

She found a stubby pencil inside her brief case, and looked around the half-moon table. The prosecutor, judge, defense attorney and guardian ad litem, all dressed in varying degrees of black and white, lent a funereal aspect to the gathering. Today she was clad in beige, a timid, neutral color to mirror her feelings.

Everything about this case was jumbled and uncertain, Christa thought. First there were the parents — so young and inexperienced, so naive. Could they hurt this baby again through their ignorance?

And then there was Tony, as tenacious a young guardian as she'd ever seen. Her initial anger while visiting the hospital had turned to surprise, then complete wonder two weeks later as she'd learned about the rescue, the flight and Tony's meticulous care of the little infant he called Jake.

Yet she knew the Department's policy: Place a child with his biological family whenever possible.

Once more, she was caught in the middle.

Suddenly she straightened, clicked her pen and wrote furiously. Whipping the paper from its tablet, she folded it quickly and handed it to Carver's attorney.

Sam Bella frowned, scanning the note. He pursed his lips, holding Christa with a steady gaze.

"Mr. Bella, we are waiting." Judge Bickle shook one arm free from her robe and fingered her wooden gavel.

Bella straightened slowly, then took a sharp breath. "Mr. Adams, do you love your baby?"

Carver's mouth opened slightly. No one had ever asked him that before. He paused, thinking of his own father — rigid, scowling, distant . . . unreachable. What should he say? *Tell the truth. Always tell the truth on the witness stand*, his attorney had coached him. He shifted, stared out the window at a starling perched on the low-topped building across the alley.

"If you mean do I feel like I love him . . . I . . . I don't know." He paused, looked straight at Marianna, so tiny and vulnerable in the pink blouse she'd bought at Wal-Mart the night before, one hand dabbing at her nose with a soggy tissue. "But I will care for him. I will make a home for us."

He squared his shoulders, gripped the arms of his chair. "I will work at McDonalds for as long as it takes. If that's what you mean by love, then yes . . . yes, I do love him."

"No further questions, your honor."

There was a murmur and a movement like grass bending to the wind as the assembled attorneys, guardian and witnesses whispered their relief. Three minutes to twelve.

Judge Bickle gave a light tap of her gavel. "We will convene again at two o'clock."

Phillip Brandon from the County Attorney's office smoothed one plump, soft hand across his tie, then rubbed a slim pen against his cheek. Marianna stared in fascination. She had never seen anyone hold a pen like a telephone.

"Mrs. Adams, why did you succumb to the cesarean?"

"Su . . . what?" Marianna wrinkled her brow.

"Why did you let the doctor take your baby by cesarean section?"

"I . . . don't know." She could see him smiling faintly, ready to pounce. "I mean, he didn't tell me . . . everything."

"This child was clearly a viable fetus."

"Vi . . . ?"

Brandon jiggled his arms into place across his ample mid-section, as if to hold himself in check. "Viable. It means he was able to live outside the womb."

"The doctor told my mother that the baby was dying. He took an ultrasound."

"And did you seek a second opinion?" Phillip lowered the pen to rub his chin and leaned back in his chair.

"Well I. . . . My mother said I should see Dr. Quaid. And I . . . I've known him since I was a little girl. I . . . believed him."

She looked at her husband. Carver was rigid, arms folded tightly across his chest.

She straightened, then flipped back her hair in one angry motion. "How can you ask me a question like that? You weren't there. All I know is that I loved my baby then and I love him now. I was just following the doctor's orders."

Her eyes narrowed. "The doctor told me it wasn't just the baby who was dying. He said that I could die, too." Her shoulders had begun to sag again, but her eyes still glittered dangerously.

"And did you ask to see the dying baby, seek to determine whether it was really dead?"

"Objection." Bella lifted one hand in a lazy motion. "Third trimester abortion for reasons of the mother's emotional and mental health is legal in this state." He glanced briefly at his watch. "And he's badgering my client."

"No further questions."

Judge Bickle shifted in her chair and scowled at the assembled attorneys and onlookers as she wielded her gavel, ready to strike.

Henry was still in town. Veda was off in the woods somewhere, and the cattle were pastured far over the hill. Tony set his meager sack of belongings near the garden path and strolled towards the walnut tree.

His father would be here soon to take him home. He'd said his goodbyes to Henry and Molly, and now it was time for one last farewell. He stood under the ancient tree and took in long breaths of cool, damp air and fragrance as new as the center of a forest.

For the first time in his life, he did not feel alone.

35

Two days had stretched into one week. Then ten days. Then two weeks. Marianna and Carver had held their baby six more times. And six more times they had watched him leave the DHS building in someone else's arms.

Judge Bickle told them she'd have a decision "soon."

But how long would they have to wait? Nobody seemed to know. Nobody seemed to care. And nobody could tell them how to deal with their latest fear — that Tony Kowalski would fight for guardianship.

In the tiny apartment above Ricky's Bar and Grille, Mr. and Mrs. Adams had made their home. Three rooms and a bath overlooking the parking lot and Rupert's Fix-it Shop. Five hundred and twenty square feet in which to live, to eat, to sleep — and hopefully to raise a baby. Their only furniture: a wobbly formica kitchen table, two chairs, a broken down sofa — and a mammoth bedroom set courtesy of Helene Morrow.

The government had taken the rest of Helene's possessions through the Rico Act. There was nothing left now to suggest further inheritance for her only daughter. Helene was bankrupt and facing trial for a number of offenses — among them illegal drug importation through her antique dealership — coupled with conspiracy to commit murder. That would do for starters.

Former Mayor Furman Adams, free on bail, had somehow managed to slip north into Canada. For his oldest son, he had left behind a legacy of debts and a soiled family name.

In the kitchen, an anemic pair of hamburger patties bubbled in the frying pan they'd bought from Goodwill. Marianna had neglected to thaw them out. Instead she had covered them with water and brought the entire mess to a boil.

Behind the stove a daunting array of barbeque sauces and Mexican condiments stood ready to conquer.

Barefoot and in blue jeans, Marianna emptied her latest purchase onto the bed. Three pairs of socks for Carver, a sweatshirt for herself, and a Pooh Bear cup for the baby she still called Little Bits. Somehow she could not bring herself to call him "Jake." That was Tony Kowalski's name for her baby.

The bathroom door opened, and Carver hurried across the hallway in a fog of steam.

"Sorry, Baby. I'm late for work." He stepped into the bedroom and began pulling sticky labels off his socks.

He sat on the bed, smoothing the new white cotton around his long legs. He winked at her. "Thanks for these."

"I'm cooking lunch . . . . Can't you wait a little longer. . . ?"

Carver shook his head, then finished dressing and mumbled his inventory: "Billfold . . . belt . . . jacket . . . ."

"Car keys. . . ." He looked around in mock confusion. "*Wife!*" He pulled Marianna close and she buried her head against his crisp white shirt with the McDonalds emblem over the pocket.

She inhaled the scent of his anti-perspirant. "M-m-m. Wish I could go with you."

He stepped back and held her hand against his cheek for a moment. "This won't last forever, Baby, I promise."

He tilted up her chin and kissed her nose. "Close the door tightly behind me. Pull the chain in place."

One hand was already on the doorknob. "Remember now. Don't let anyone in."

The door clicked behind him and she could hear his footsteps on the faded floor boards, then the creak of the second step, followed by an accelerated light tapping as Carver ran down the stairs.

Marianna wiped her eyes. She would miss him, yes, but the worst thing was the incredible boredom. Every morning Carver stumped the city looking for a better job. Then, home for a quick lunch, a change of clothes, and a hurried goodbye before his McDonald's shift.

And so it went day after day. No one to talk to. Her friends were in school or on the athletic field. And her mother . . . well. . . .

She looked around the room. Maybe she shouldn't have urged Carver to stuff their bedroom with that hulking bed and dresser set. Helene's polished cherrywood furniture, jammed against the west wall, stretched a few inches past the doorway and nearly covered the window.

Marianna leaned across the dresser and glanced outside. A half dozen shriveled leaves hung tenaciously to the lone tree in the parking lot. Already it was nearing the end of October, and now she would have to wait until January to go back to school.

Each day she tormented herself with questions. If by some miracle they finally brought their baby home, who would babysit? Could they afford to pay someone?

Oh, if only she could just talk things over with Carver. But for the past two weeks he'd come home from McDonald's at seven-thirty every night, too exhausted to speak. After a quick stretch on the sofa, he would open the laptop and work on his thesis until nearly midnight.

The only time they had together was in the car — two hours of driving back and forth between Cedar Bend and Colchester three times a week — just to spend one hour with their baby.

A knock at the door. Soft at first, then repeated. Marianna stepped cautiously from the bedroom, then peered through the tiny peephole. Outside a man stood with his head turned towards the stairs. Should she let him in? No. Carver was firm: Never open the door to strangers.

Another soft knock, then he turned his face. She'd seen him before — at one of the hearings. She unbolted the door and opened it a few inches, keeping the chain in place.

He was short and slim, his dark curls framing a troubled face.

Sudden recognition widened her eyes. She wanted to slam the door and bolt it, shutting him out for all eternity. Instead she stood gripping the knob, making no move to close the door or to open it.

"Okay if I talk to you? Just for a minute?"

Marianna stood uncertainly for a few moments, then released the chain and opened the door. As Tony stepped in, she moved back defensively and motioned to one of the kitchen chairs. "You can . . . you can sit . . . if you like."

Tony moved the chair closer to the wall, as far away from her as possible in this doll-sized room. Embarrassed, he looked past Marianna to the tiny window behind the sink. Finally she sat in the other chair, pressing herself against the other wall. They eyed each other cautiously.

"I never wanted to think about you." His voice was low and flat. "But after awhile that's all I *could* think about. How you . . . how you must have felt when you finally knew the truth." He rested his hands in his lap, lacing his fingers. Marianna's eyes softened. She lifted a napkin off the table and began scrunching it.

"Jake and I . . . ." Tony's voice caught. "Jake and I . . . well, I thought for awhile . . . that is, I hoped . . . that Jake and my father and I . . . that we could be a family." He pressed his fingertips against his forehead, still looking down. "But now I know that God had something else in mind."

Marianna still had not spoken, her wadded napkin at the ready.

He cleared his throat, looked steadily at Marianna, hoping for a response. She sat rigid, her hands folded tightly.

Tony plunged ahead. "He's your child. You both . . . I mean you and Carver . . . I really think you love him. . . . I know that now. He was only mine to rescue."

Tony held her gaze for a moment, then looked down again, focusing on his stained boots. "I . . . I will not fight for custody of Jake."

A sudden intake of breath startled him. Marianna moved her head slowly from side to side, a single tear slipping towards her chin.

Tony didn't know what to do. The need to comfort her was overwhelming, but he stayed fast to his chair. Marianna had already used up the first napkin, and was groping for reinforcements. Still she did not speak, and the two sat quietly in the tiny kitchen for a handful of minutes, listening to the sound of shared breathing.

Marianna spoke first, her words brittle and tight and just a little too loud, as if she were trying to keep herself from flying to pieces.

"We don't deserve him. We haven't done anything to show that we deserve him." She was shocked by her own statement. What was she saying! Certainly she had not meant to show weakness to this guy, of all people!

Tony leaned back in the chair, hoping his stillness would keep her tears in check. "If we all got what we deserved, none of us would have anything," he said.

Marianna looked at him with widening eyes.

"Maybe you think you won't be very good parents. That's what I thought — at first. I just couldn't seem to do anything right. It took me awhile to realize that God had put one great teacher right in my path and most of what I know I learned by watching him."

Marianna, too muffled in napkins to speak, simply raised one eyebrow to signal her question.

"It was Jake. He was my teacher." Tony smiled and put out his hand. "I don't mean I did whatever he wanted. That's not it at all." He got up slowly, walked a couple of steps to the sink. "I realize now that it was God who helped me see what Jake needed."

Man, he was beginning to feel dumb. Marianna was just sitting there with a stack of kitchen napkins jammed against her face. He'd try again.

"It's like this. God was always right there, wanting to show me what Jake was like inside, what he was thinking, what would help him grow. "

Once more he sensed the questions behind those eyebrows. "That's different, you know — different from giving him everything he wants. It's giving him what he *needs*."

He paused, then took a deep breath and plunged ahead. "And now I know — I really know — that what Jake needs is you. He needs you and Carver. You are his mother and father. And . . . and you love him. I knew it, deep down, that day in the courtroom when you were both up there on the stand."

Still no response. The napkins were beginning to leak around the edges. Tony tried a different tack. "I used to dance with Jake. We'd take my mother's old Spanish tapes and dance all over the apartment."

He crossed his arms and fixed his gaze on the grease-encrusted ceiling fan. "And you know, I never felt better than when I was dancing with that little guy." He glanced at her again and was rewarded with a grudging smile.

Marianna wiped her nose and put down most of the napkins, her head tilted slightly as she listened to Tony.

"Well, it's something like that. Raising Jake, I mean. It's sort of like a dance, with God doing the leading. I just had to make sure I listened to his music."

Marianna was so quiet it was beginning to rattle him. More breathing. More quiet spaces. More, perhaps, than Tony could handle. Maybe he should just keep talking. At least she wasn't telling him to stop.

"I didn't know all this until after I took Jake out to see the cows that day." Now he was in for it, bringing up that stupid stunt. Marianna would get mad, send him packing. But she just sat huddled against the wall, staring at him.

"I've told everyone in the world that I'm sorry, especially God . . . but I haven't told you," he finished softly.

On sudden impulse he leaned across the table and touched her hand. "Marianna, I'm really, really sorry that I hurt your baby. Henry was always warning me not to take Jake out there but I did it anyway."

She took up her stack of napkins again, but to her surprise she did not need them. An immense calm had settled over her like a mantle. She smiled and looked away, a little frown working across her face.

"The only thing you did wrong was try to . . . to have some fun with Jake . . . and maybe . . . maybe you did try to be macho. Lots of guys do that."

More quiet, as if she were listening for something, then, "But what I did — I should have known better."

Tony sat motionless.

"Doctor Quaid hurt my mother a long time ago. And my mother . . . . I think . . . I think she was using me to get back at him. I know that now."

Marianna slumped, staring into space, digging far into a dark memory. "I tried to fool myself. I told myself the doctor was right, but deep inside I think I really knew the truth about our baby."

She scowled. Then, her voice raspy and bitter — "I was too chicken or too scared or too dumb to do anything about it."

The words echoed in the kitchen, hunting for answers. The two of them had stopped talking, an unspoken truce filling the silent places.

Marianna's next words were like soft slaps. "You were just showing off with Jake, but I nearly killed my baby. And — and maybe . . . maybe, you know, I think somehow I knew what I was doing."

She breathed one deep sob.

Tony took both of her hands — how tiny they were! "Marianna, that doesn't change anything for me. I still want you and Carver to have your baby."

Her eyes widened. She released her hands and turned towards the window, afraid to look at him.

Tony laughed softly. "Just now you did what it took me nineteen years to do. You told the real truth to someone besides yourself."

Marianna turned her head back towards Tony and lifted her wad of napkins again, wiping her eyes and trembling. She held her gaze steady, smiling through her tears.

Then she began to laugh, softly at first, her shaky voice punctuated by sobs.

Tony watched her awhile, enjoying her freedom. "The next thing you can do," he whispered, "is tell God the truth."

Marianna wiped her nose and eyes. They sat quietly, stealing shy glances at each other. Every once in awhile she let go with a tiny laugh.

"Hey, Marianna, did Jake ever go like this?" Tony squashed his features into a turtle face, then moved his arms in little erratic jerks.

Marianna giggled. "Yeah. Yeah, he did. And oh boy can he make weird noises!"

Tony slapped the table. Yeah, like this: "Shlbphth!" He blew a couple of raspberries.

"I think you *have* been learning from him!"

Marianna's laughter diminished to a smile.

Tony picked up a napkin and absently began to wipe the already clean table, looking at the wall, the window, uncomfortable again with looking at her.

"Tony, would you . . . could I get you a soda or something?"

Tony shook his head and got up. He glanced at his watch. "I said I'd just stay a minute." He flashed a brief smile. It's time for me to go."

Marianna put down her napkins and followed him to the door. "Hey . . . ."

He turned back, one hand resting on the doorknob.

"In the courtroom I heard that little girl call you Uncle Tony." She reached out and touched his sleeve. "Will you. . . . I mean could you . . . be Jake's Uncle Tony?"

He laughed. "Yeah. . . . Yeah, that's me. Uncle Tony."

In the alley his steps were quick and light, and he whistled as he walked towards the little white car that was once the center of his life. He paused, running his hands over the cold, hard fender.

Then he slapped the metal twice and swung into the canvas-topped Jeep. A quick turn of the key and the buggy purred to life, picking up speed on Fourth Street.

Two more miles and there was Shannon Memorial on his left, its emergency entrance perched at the top of the hill. In six hours he would return for the night shift.

Up the street, two more blocks.

Now the red light at Hubbard Avenue.

He leaned his arm out the window and patted the door to a tune in his head, then slipped a CD into his new stereo. A soft whoosh and the disc settled into place.

A green light, the muffled whine of softly revved motors, the far-away thunder of kettle drums.

Then, a vast chorus of violins erupted as Beethoven's Ninth Symphony accompanied Tony all the way home to his father's house.

Acknowledgements

Many friends, family members and professionals walked with me as this story took shape. It was a walk I could not have taken alone. Their advice was sound, so I take all the blame for the poetic twists.

My humble thanks to:

Law Enforcement: Kim Griffith; Steve Haefner; Bill Hermas; Jeff Olson.

Medical: Marcia Michaelsen; Sheri Nussbaum; R. W. Fischer.

Department of Human Services: Lauren Holst.

Ranching: Dave Lubben; Ron Niemann; Bill Larson.

Proofreading, prayer and encouragement: Jennie and Joe Rosio; Erik and Jeanene Carlson; Mark and Stephanie Larson; Bill and Laura Hendrick; Kathleen and David Barlow; Susan and Paul Sturges; Forrest Dolgener; Glenn Carlson; Glen and Carolyn Confer; Wanda Bailey; Susan Stanley; Sue Heth; Judy Frey; Arlen Foster; Peter Marshall; Lori Palmer; Pacesetters ABF; Barb Anderson; Merton Clarkson; Steve and Nancy Larson; Stacie Holmes; Chris Rygh; Forrest Dolgener; Kay Fuller; Pat Cleigh; Caylin Cervetti; Julie Smithson; Hilda Ostby; Jeannine Becker; Dee Schildroth; Ruth Ewig; Alessandra Mercon; Amy Dolgener; Ed Puterbaugh; Gene Logsdon; Bev Owen; Clementine Msengi; Mark and Shonda Kuiper; Rick and Sue Shaw; Chris and Holly Fleshner.

Prayer, encouragement, advice — and boldly going where no one else has gone: Alice Dolgener.

My husband, my dearest friend — and the best writer I know: Jerry Carlson.